THE
DOCTOR'S
WIFE

THE DOCTOR'S WIFE

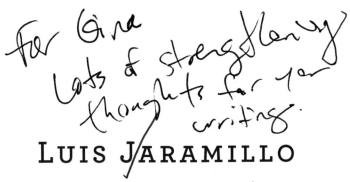

For Gina
Lots of strengthening
thoughts for your
writing.

LUIS JARAMILLO

Brooklyn, NY

2017

db
DZANC
BOOKS

DZANC BOOKS

5220 Dexter Ann Arbor Rd.
Ann Arbor, MI 48103
www.dzancbooks.org

THE DOCTOR'S WIFE

Published 2012 by Dzanc Books
Book Design by Steven Seighman
Cover design by Amanda Jane Jones
Cover photo by Jessica Antola

ISBN: 978-1-938103-56-8
Third edition: APril 2014

ART WORKS.
arts.gov

*michigan council for
arts and cultural affairs*

This project is supported in part by an award from
the National Endowment for the Arts and MCACA.

Printed in the United States of America

10 9 8 7 6 5 4 3

For GMD

Contents

PART II

PART I

Expecting

The Doctor's Wife is pregnant with her fourth child.

The Woods

It's after lunch, and the Doctor's Wife has given Ann and her siblings two packets of saltine crackers each and told them to play hard until she calls them for dinner.

Ann thinks that's fine. She doesn't want to be inside. On stormy spring days like this, the lake roils with inky waves and becomes the Atlantic Ocean. The world is in black and white like a newsreel. It's up to Ann and her siblings to defend the United States against the Germans. The three kids have white-blond hair, blue eyes, and their last name is Hagen. Do they care that this is a German name? No.

They prepare for the grim battle. Bob is 10, Ann is 8 and Chrissy is 6. They drag the overturned metal fishing boat into position on the sand and now the boat is a bunker. The pieces of driftwood around the fire pit become a jail for the POWs. Ace, their black Labrador retriever, keeps dropping a wet stick at Ann's feet and wagging his tail, but he is really a military police dog. Bob props oars against the boat, shoving the paddles into the sand and pointing the handles out to sea, so that the Americans have cannons with which to hit the approaching destroyers.

But the German attack is brutal.

"Retreat!" Bob yells. Ann runs, feeling the hot, fetid breath of the enemy behind her. She runs past the house, down the driveway, across the street and into the woods, pushing through the jungle of blackberry bushes, pine saplings. She turns past the hermit's shack, stomping on ferns, pushing aside alder shoots tangling under the canopy of Douglas firs.

Ann meets her siblings at the tree house, a ramshackle collection of boards they've wedged in the crotch of a giant tree. Bob calls down for the other two to hurry up and climb, but Chrissy's been hit by a bullet. Ann, now a nurse, kneels over her sister's sprawled body, pressing ferns into her wounds to stanch the bleeding.

"I'm better now," Chrissy says, leaping up. The kids run from the Germans again, fleeing toward the swamp, crossing the creek on the pieces of plywood they've made into bridges. In the swamp, Ann picks a skunk cabbage and flings it past Chrissy's head toward the enemy. Chrissy stops, gagging at the smell. Ann doesn't know why Chrissy has to always behave so dramatically. It must be her youth.

"Let's hunt for frogs," Bob says, and the Germans are forgotten. Ann uses a stick to push aside the pussy willows. Chrissy lunges for one frog, clumsily and too loudly. It's Bob who first catches one, cupping it in his hands. He opens his hand enough so that they can see it.

"What are we going to do with it?" Ann asks.

"Keep it?" Chrissy asks.

Bob shakes his head, placing the frog gently down onto a dry patch, where it hops off into the reeds. They wipe their hands on their pants and unwrap the saltines. Ann licks the little bits of salt off the surface of her cracker.

After they're done with their snack, Bob dares Ann to knock on the hermit's door. There isn't anything definitively bad about the hermit, but what you don't know you make up, and Ann can imagine plenty. She shakes a little as she taps the door.

The hermit answers Ann's knock. She tries to peer past him into his house, but sees only dark and shadows. He reaches into his pocket, pulling out a handful of butterscotches, the hard kind wrapped in yellow cellophane. Ann extends her hand to receive the gift.

Then the Doctor's Wife is calling for them, her loud voice telling them to come in to dinner. They run back home through the woods, stopping when they get to the street to divide the candy evenly. When they're in the kitchen setting the table, Chrissy pops a butterscotch in her mouth.

"Where did you get that?" their mother asks, and Chrissy is dumb enough to tell her.

The Doctor's Wife becomes very angry.

The Sewer

The Doctor's Wife is dressing for a dance at the Everett Country Club. She's made her own dress, a simple black silk thing she hopes looks acceptable. She looks in the mirror at a side angle to see if it works or not. She smoothes down the fabric over her belly. "Can you tell?" she asks.

"Not exactly," the Doctor says, knotting his tie.

The doorbell rings. The Doctor's Wife slips on her left pump as she hop skips down the stairs. Hazel Adelsheim is at the door, here to take care of the kids. She's a blowsy sort of woman, scattered. Her husband is a real bastard.

"They need to be in bed by nine at the very latest," the Doctor's Wife says. Hazel waves her out the door.

The Doctor and the Doctor's Wife drive through a light drizzle, over the trestle above the Snohomish River and Ebey Slough. The drawbridge, which the Doctor's Wife has never seen drawn, looks down over logging barges underneath. The wipers sweep the glass, the lights of other cars forming weird shapes in the wet swiping. In Everett, they turn at the sign for the club, up the drive. The clubhouse is clad in dark gray siding. The whole building needs to be replaced or at least rehabbed. The Doctor likes to golf and is good at it. The

Doctor's Wife occasionally walks around the course and knocks the ball into the bushes.

Under the porte cochère, the Doctor opens the door of their Plymouth, helping her out of the car. She doesn't need the help but she takes his hand. Inside, she shakes out her coat and hands it to the attendant, heading upstairs.

"Where did you get that dress?" Nancy Taylor asks when the Doctor and the Doctor's Wife walk into the banquet room.

"Oh, you know," the Doctor's Wife says.

"Seattle? I won't tell your hubby how many hundreds of dollars you spent," Nancy stage whispers.

"Thousands," the Doctor's Wife says.

Nancy shakes her head as understanding comes. "You made it yourself, you dirty dog! Everything I try to sew turns out looking like a flour sack." Nancy is more of a craft person than a seamstress. She likes to make Santa and Mrs. Clauses out of pine cones and that sort of thing. Nancy narrows her eyes. "But it's not just the dress. Something's different about you."

"There isn't either," The Doctor's Wife says, not liking to lie, but she's not ready to tell her best friend. The older three kids were born almost exactly two years apart from each other.

"Have you lost weight? Haircut?"

"How many people do you have lined up for the meeting?" the Doctor's Wife asks.

"Fine, don't tell me," Nancy says. "I have a solid five."

Jim Taylor puts his arm around his wife. "You gals better get us some sewers. I'm tired of digging up the drain field on the nastiest day of the year."

"I'm tired of having you complain about it," Nancy drawls back. The truth is that everybody is sick of dealing with the septic systems. At least the Taylors and the Hagens have septic tanks. From some houses a pipe pumps raw sewage directly into the lake. A few years ago, after horrible smelling algae bloomed in the lake, the Doctor started taking samples three times a week, sending them to the

Snohomish County Health Department. The levels of coliform bacterium were at a count of 1,000 per 100 mL of tested water, four times the amount considered safe for drinking, and high enough so that the lake should have been closed for swimming. The county wouldn't do anything about the bacteria. Over the past year, the Doctor's Wife and Nancy have worked with the Community Development Bureau of the University of Washington to establish a sewer district. That was part one of the battle. Part two is to convince homeowners that it's in their own best interests to vote for the bond issue to fund the sewer.

"You know what Greta Sorenson told me? She's swum in the lake for fifty years and she's never been bothered. She's never had typhoid and nobody she's known has had typhoid, so why do we need sewers?" Nancy says.

"What did you say to her?" the Doctor's Wife asks.

"I told her, 'This community is going nowhere without a sewer. If you don't help out, then don't ever bitch to me about getting a dentist to come to town.'"

"Some people aren't as bright as the two of us."

"No," Nancy cackles.

But Greta isn't the only problem. The people on the hill say things like, "I don't live on the lake, so why should I have to pay?" She knows that some think that she and Nancy are rich bastards twisting people's arms to make them cough up money they don't have. But this is a gross distortion of the facts. The Doctor's Wife grew up in the Depression, and she knows what it is to count a penny. But money isn't God. Even God isn't God as far as the Doctor's Wife is concerned.

"I'll tell you one thing, it'll be a fight to convince these people to vote for the bond issue," the Doctor's Wife says to Nancy.

"If I have to go to every house," Nancy says.

"Me too," the Doctor's Wife says, feeling a competitive twinge.

The Doctor, standing with Jim and the other men suddenly turns, winking at his wife. "A dance?" he asks.

"We're conferring," she says, but she's pleased.

"Go on ahead, my shoes pinch anyway," Nancy says, rolling her eyes about Jim, who's busy telling a story to a crowd. The Doctor leads the Doctor's Wife to the dance floor.

"I think you live across the street from me," the Doctor had said, cutting in, the first time they ever spoke. On Fridays in the summer, the student union of the University of Kansas blocked off streets on campus, strung up Chinese lanterns, put down a dance floor and hired a big band to play.

"Is that so?" she'd replied.

But the truth was, she'd had her eye on him. Every morning from the parlor of her sorority house she watched him leaving his rooming house across the street toting a microscope, the case slung over her shoulder, held tight against his tall, skinny body.

She can feel the Doctor's ribs through his blazer as they dance on the small dance floor set up by the windows overlooking the fairway. The Doctor's Wife tells herself that the kids are getting ready for bed at home.

(They are not. They have not even brushed their teeth or washed their faces. They are playing a rambunctious game with Hazel—a grownup—chasing each other through a burrow built of sofa pillows, blankets, and overturned chairs.)

Rounds

This morning they've already had to go to church and now Chrissy is waiting in the car with her mother and siblings for the Doctor to finish his rounds at Providence, the second hospital of the morning.

Chrissy watches the clouds, wondering how her life will change when she's no longer the youngest. There are pros and cons. She'll be able to dress the baby, but the baby will probably cry a lot. The baby might be stinky, and Chrissy has a very sensitive nose.

Chrissy tries to amuse herself by nibbling off the offending edge of her left thumbnail.

"You know what's going to happen?" Ann asks quietly.

"Happen with what?" Chrissy asks as she tears off a satisfying piece of nail with her teeth.

"The fibers of your fingernails are going to form a big ball in your stomach and the ball will stay there until you die."

The piece of nail lodges in her throat. She has absolutely no doubt that what Ann says is true. There are consequences for her actions, usually unpleasant ones for anything actually fun. But what else was she supposed to do with the chewed bits? If she spit them out, her mother would not be happy. Chrissy wonders how large the ball is already. As big as a gumball? An egg? The nerves of the situation keep her chewing.

The Doctor's Wife works the crossword in the newspaper in the front seat. Bob leafs through a comic book. Ann is reading too, looking disgustingly smug. Chrissy tries to wrestle the book out of Ann's hands. Ann screams.

"I'll give a quarter to the child who stays quietest the longest," the Doctor's Wife says briskly.

Chrissy returns to her nails. That is at least a quiet activity and she could use a quarter. Chrissy feels Ann's finger jab her right ribs.

"She's touching me!" Chrissy shrieks, bucking back into Bob.

"Knock it off," he says, pushing her the other way.

Ann smiles at her, remaining silent. She's won the quarter, the beast. She won't even buy candy like anybody sensible would. She'll just squirrel it away and lord it over Chrissy.

Out of the corner of her eye, she sees a flash as the glass door to the parking lot catches the sun.

"You took forever," Chrissy says when the Doctor lets himself into the car.

"Let me smell your breath," the Doctor's Wife says. "Just as I suspected. Having coffee with the doctors again!"

"And probably the nurses too!" Chrissy says.

"Yes, probably," the Doctor's Wife says, swatting the Doctor's bottom as he sits.

How unappealing!

Boys

The Doctor's Wife knows her husband to be a person somewhat fixated on safety. For example, if the Doctor sees somebody speeding or driving erratically, he'll say, "I'll see you at the hospital later." He's always prepared to go fishing, a pole and flies at the ready in the car. But in case he has a heart attack while fishing—this is how his own father died, wading in a river, fishing pole in hand—he brings along a few pills of Valium (the drug calms the frantic patient) and Canadian Club whiskey in a flask (to act as a quick anticoagulant). Under no circumstances is anybody allowed to eat a cream pie from a restaurant. And speaking of restaurants, if the family is on a road trip and the silverware looks at all grimy, even if they've been driving for hours in hundred degree weather and it's air conditioned in the restaurant, the doctor will force the whole family to march in a humiliating parade back to the hot car to find a more hygienic establishment.

So it is very surprising when one morning that summer, the Doctor allows Bob to keep a live bat he claims he found "sleeping" in the front yard. "I think there's a cage in the basement," the Doctor says with a shrug.

The Doctor's Wife gives a look to her husband as the kids run out of the kitchen making more noise than you could think three kids could make. She feels the baby kick.

"I thought it would keep them out of your hair," he says. The Doctor's Wife sincerely hopes that neither the children nor the bat will be injured. She isn't a fatalist, not yet anyway.

In the basement, Bob eases the bat down on the floor of the cage. His sisters hang back, refusing to get near the cage, where the bat lies prone, its wings drawn around itself. Bob shows his sisters how he's not afraid to take the bat out of its cage and pet its head.

"What if it's rabid?" asks Ann.

"Let me hold it," says Chrissy, grabbing at the animal, seeming to forget her initial fear. She tries to tug at the little claws at the end of the wings. "Why won't it open them? Now it just looks like a mouse."

"It's daytime, so it's sleeping," Bob says. "Dummy."

Bob takes the bat back from Chrissy and sets it in the cage. He's pretty sure the bat isn't rabid.

"Do you think it's a boy or a girl?"

"I can't see anything," Bob says.

"I mean the baby."

"I hope it's a boy. I'm tired of so many girls," Bob says.

"I hope it's a boy too," says Chrissy, squinting her eyes at Ann.

Gretel

The Doctor comes home with a German Shorthaired Pointer puppy he's already named Gretel. The Doctor's wife is assured that the puppy will be the Doctor's responsibility. The kids are thrilled about the new dog and immediately start to play with her. The Doctor's Wife narrowly saves Gretel from being made to wear a doll's dress.

A week after she has joined the family, Gretel is feverish, won't eat, and her eye oozes with pus. She coughs, has a fever, and vomits in her cardboard box in the basement.

"Your puppy is sick," the Doctor's Wife says when she calls her husband's office. Hazel Adelsheim is upstairs helping out with the kids. The Doctor's Wife had planned on chairing a sewer meeting with Nancy.

"You're going to have to pull double duty today," she says to Nancy on the phone.

"What's wrong?"

"You don't want to know."

"Kid?"

"*Dog*," the Doctor's Wife says.

"It doesn't look good," the vet says. He's a fishing buddy of the Doctor's. "Such a pretty little dog too. She has diphtheria. Dogs don't really ever get better from it. Even if they live, the encephalitis can cause bad trouble with the brain and the muscles. Any treatment would be only supportive. Want me to put her down?"

No, neither the Doctor nor the Doctor's Wife want that.

Gretel pants heavily in a cardboard box in the kitchen, whimpering. It's an awful noise, so full of suffering that the kids steer clear of the box, playing quietly upstairs. The Doctor is called away to Providence for an emergency, but she and the Doctor work as a team. She can't just let that little dog die.

She uses an eyedropper to keep Gretel hydrated. She wipes pus from Gretel's eyes, she cleans out the cardboard box as it becomes soiled, she puts cold clothes on the hot doggy body. This goes on for days until the Doctor's Wife starts to think that maybe it would have been better to allow the vet to do as he suggested.

But Gretel lives.

The Lake

Chrissy gobbles down her lunch, hoping that today the Doctor's Wife will forget her rule that they wait half an hour to get in the water. She doesn't forget.

"It's boring to wait," Chrissy wails.

"If you're bored, I'll give you something to do," her mother says brightly.

Ann gives Chrissy a poisonous look. Everybody receives assignments. Ann's job is to vacuum and Chrissy's is to dust. All Bob has to do is take out the trash. The trash will only take two seconds and the vacuuming is easy too. Dusting will take years. Chrissy is prepared to rebel, but then an interesting thing happens. The Doctor's Wife walks quickly into the downstairs bathroom and shuts the door behind herself. Chrissy draws close enough to the door to hear a retching sound.

"Are you sick?" Chrissy asks.

The Doctor's Wife opens the door, toothbrush in mouth. "Sometimes when one is pregnant, one vomits."

"Did you throw up when you were pregnant with me?"

"Of course." She fixes her eyes on Chrissy. "Don't you have a job to do?"

Chrissy does, but she takes the long way around to the broom closet, through the kitchen instead of through the den. She opens the refrigerator and takes out two carrots. Chrissy loves carrots, crunchy and tasting of the color orange. She doesn't have time to scrape them today, and, anyway, she doesn't mind the skin. These are the first of the day, and they barely touch her hunger. She's eaten so many carrots this summer that her skin has started to turn a very pale yellow. Chrissy's goal is to turn orange.

"Right this instant," her mother says.

"I'm almost there," Chrissy replies, swallowing the last bite and entering the broom closet. Big roasting pans, splatter screens, a very large sieve and a smaller one with a black handle, a colander, and the biggest stock pot hang on hooks. Cleaning solutions including a big bottle of ammonia, Windex and Pledge sit on the middle shelf at the back of the closet. Chrissy grabs the canister of Pledge. The small vacuum cleaner used on the stairs looks like baby elephant draping its trunk over a hook. Next to the trunk hangs the stuffed bag of rags, soft and clean.

"Chrissy!" her mother says.

"I'm getting a rag," Chrissy explains, leaving the broom closet with her rag and canister of polish. In the living room she vigorously mists the top of the piano, drawing the rag over the wood and then pounding on the keys with the wadded up cloth.

"Quit banging!" Ann yells over the noise of the stand-up vacuum cleaner she runs across the carpet in front of her.

"I'm not banging," Chrissy yells back, thumping with her fist. Just because Ann can play the piano doesn't mean she should tell Chrissy what to do with the instrument. For good measure, Chrissy gives the low keys a last whack before slamming the lid and tackling what everybody calls the bone table, then all the little side tables, and then the mantle. At the bookshelf, she plops down to look at the German bible with the family names in it. Ann hits her thigh with the vacuum cleaner.

This causes yelling, tears, and the girls are sent upstairs to tidy their room peacefully.

Chrissy wads up her clothes and shoves them in her dresser drawers. Ann is so perfect that she's perfectly folding all of her clothes into prissy little rectangles. Chrissy doesn't know why she and Ann have to share a bedroom. Her grandparents only come a couple times a year—why do they need a whole bedroom to themselves? If she could have that room instead and not have to share with Ann, then she'd be happy. Chrissy's bed is lumpy, no matter how much she tries to smooth it.

"Here," Ann says, yanking the coverlet into place, and now they're done. The sun shines brightly outside. It is cruel to be kept cooped up like this. Chrissy calls her mother upstairs.

"Will it pass the white glove test?" the Doctor's Wife asks.

"Oh, yes," Chrissy says, hoping she won't look inside the drawers.

"Go outside and swim," the Doctor's Wife says.

Chrissy rips her clothes off and puts on her bathing suit, still slightly damp in the lining from the day before.

Sun Valley

The trip to Sun Valley is conceived of as a way to please everybody. There are horses. Her husband can fish. The kids can swim in the pool or go to the swimming hole down the path. There is even bowling in the lodge.

It takes over twelve hours to drive to Idaho, so they leave as the sun is rising, aiming to arrive by dinnertime. They head over the mountains, stopping for lunch in eastern Washington, at an oasis of sorts, a dark grove where they sit at a picnic table. They eat bread and butter sandwiches, pickles, and fried chicken the Doctor's Wife prepared the night before. After lunch, the Doctor's Wife stubs out her cigarette and they climb back in the car, driving through the dry heat of Eastern Washington, Yakima, and into Oregon, through Pendelton, and down through Idaho. It's very hot, and the kids start to complain. The Doctor's Wife would also like to complain. The horizon line shimmers in the distance and the hills are dry with little scrub pines.

"I have heat exhaustion," Chrissy says.

The Doctor's Wife wonders where she picked that phrase up. "If you really had heat exhaustion you couldn't talk."

Chrissy opens her mouth and lolls back against the seat.

"Let's play a game of 'In My Grandmother's Trunk,'" the Doctor's Wife says, beginning, "In my grandmother's trunk there's an argyle sock."

It's supposed to be a learning exercise. They prompt each other so that even Chrissy is able to reach to the end of the alphabet. When they're done, the Doctor's Wife looks down at her watch. This activity has taken about fifteen minutes. After about a hundred rounds of Twenty Questions, they climb up the pass though the mountains and it starts to get a bit cooler. Sun Valley spreads below.

They have three adjoining rooms in the lodge. After the luggage is carried in by all hands, the kids ask if they can go swimming.

"Of course, that's why we're here," The Doctor's Wife says, relaxing at the thought of the lifeguard at the pool.

Dinner is cowboy beans, cornbread, barbequed chicken, and salad, with gingerbread and whipped cream for dessert.

"This cooking isn't half as good as yours," the Doctor says. This is beside the point. The best thing is that the Doctor's Wife neither has to cook nor clean up. It's becoming a bit less comfortable to move around. Tomorrow she'll lounge in a deck chair and read a book. She hasn't done this in a long time.

An hour after the kids have been tucked into bed, there's a knock on the adjoining door.

The Doctor's Wife puts her book down. Ann presents her tear-streaked face. Chrissy is right next to her, dry-eyed.

"What's wrong?"

Ann shakes her head.

"Did you have a bad dream?"

No.

"Did you and your sister argue?"

No.

"Are you sick? Does your stomach hurt?"

"I want to go home," Ann says in a feeble voice.

Chrissy glares at Ann.

"Why? What's wrong?" the Doctor's Wife asks.

"I'm homesick."

"We just got here."

"I'm homesick."

"There are horses! Mom, tell her! Don't listen to her," Chrissy wails.

Ann sets her jaw.

The Doctor's Wife looks to her husband for help. "Do what you want," he says.

"It's too late to drive home tonight. We can wake up with fresh eyes tomorrow," the Doctor's Wife says, though she's witnessed Ann being stubborn before.

The next morning, Ann packs her small bag. She refuses to swim, bowl, read a book, go fishing with her father, or ride horses.

"I want to go home," she says to every suggestion. What can the Doctor's Wife do in the face of determination like that? She admires it. The next day they leave for home.

Outside

Chrissy and the others grab beach towels off the utility porch and then run down the lawn with the dogs, Ace barking and Gretel trying to keep up. Humans and dogs thunder to the end of the dock and then stop, looking down at the water. The lake is fed by cold springs and is a hundred feet deep in the center. No matter how sunny it gets, the lake stays chilly. Chrissy screws up her courage and jumps. As she hits, her heart seizes up for a second and her stomach contracts.

"It's warm today," Chrissy declares when she pops above the water.

"Hot," Ann confirms.

They scramble up the slippery steps of the ladder to leap off the dock and into the water, over and over. They are crazy, they are different characters, kicking out and splashing down. Chrissy can feel herself growing colder, especially on the dock. The wind has picked up, pushing the water into waves that catch sunlight, chilling it in the process. But it isn't bad as long as she keeps moving, keeps jumping. The wind can't touch her if she's completely underwater. She opens her eyes underwater, pretending she's a shark, swimming to eat her sister. She clamps on to Ann's ankle with her right hand.

Ann kicks away, swimming to the ladder, Chrissy in hot pursuit. They leap in again and this time Ann chases Chrissy.

They swim until they are all three blue and their mother calls them in for lunch. Chrissy ignores the first call. Ann, who always does what she is told, says, "Come on!"

"One more jump," Chrissy says. And still she lingers, swimming in toward the shallows. This is vastly preferable than walking back along the exposed dock. She swims until she can feel pebbles on her belly. The water barely covers her, and she is at the ladder to the deck in front of the cabana. She stands part way up and then hunches under the dock, lifting a heavy rock. A crawfish shoots backward between her legs. "I need a bucket," Chrissy yells at Ann. "I found crawdads."

"They're always there. You need to get out of the water," Ann replies. Chrissy climbs up the ladder and wraps a towel around herself.

The sun shines fully, beating down on the lawn. The wind is blocked by the trees. Chrissy trains her eyes on the grass, trying to find a bee to trap in her cupped palms. She loves the electrical feel of the buzzing in her hands, but the trick is to catch and release before being stung. She's been stung many times this summer. In a patch of clover Chrissy finds a huge bumblebee, slow moving, easy prey. She catches it, feeling the fur tickle her palms.

"Hurry up, slow poke," Ann says, her hands on her hips. Chrissy lets the bee go, free to return to his hive. Chrissy wishes she didn't have to go indoors.

"Can we take sleeping bags and sleep down on the beach tonight?" Bob asks when they sit down for lunch.

"Yes, can we?" Chrissy asks.

"We'll see," the Doctor's Wife says.

"May we spend the night on the beach?" Bob asks again at the dinner table.

"Sure," the Doctor says.

"Take your elbows off the table," the Doctor's Wife says.

Chrissy's not worrying about what she's eating, mechanically shoving in the steamed broccoli, a roasted chicken thigh, big gulps of milk, and peach cobbler for dessert. After Chrissy and Ann finish washing and drying the dinner dishes, Chrissy and the others load up the wheelbarrow with wood and steer it down the front lawn. Bob and the Doctor build a fire in the pit on the beach. The Doctor's Wife brings marshmallows down and once those have been eaten, her parents go back up to the house.

Chrissy and the others stretch sleeping bags out on the lawn, close to the fire. Small waves lap the shore. Chrissy looks at the Milky Way, a white smudge across the black sky. Bats flit around above her, lots of them. She's never slept entirely outdoors before. Once in Yellowstone, they were in a tent and the Doctor had to bang pots together to make a bear go away. Now there is no tent, no pots, and no dad. Chrissy hasn't even seen any bears nor has she heard about bears around here but that doesn't mean that there aren't any. Chrissy hears something splashing in the water. It sounds big and like it might be climbing up the sand. Chrissy is terrified, but she doesn't want to be teased. She doesn't say anything as she scoots her sleeping bag as close as she can to Ann's.

"What are you doing?"

"I'm cold."

"Are you scared?"

"No."

"Ace will protect us," Ann says confidently.

Ann knows everything and sometimes this is a good thing. What she says is true. They are safe because Ace guards them, sitting like a sphinx.

In the morning, the sleeping bags are damp from the dew and Chrissy is woken up by the rhythmic licking of Ace's tongue on her face.

Bond Issue I

Nancy Taylor and the Doctor's Wife perch on the sofa in front of the television camera. Frank Anderson from the Community Development Bureau sits in an armchair close by. There's real coffee in the coffee pot and it's Nancy's job to pour cups for everybody three minutes into the show.

"Just talk to each other naturally, as if you were at home," the producer, a man from Channel 9 says.

"Naturally?" Nancy asks. "We'd better get the kids here too, then."

"And the dogs," the Doctor's Wife says.

"I'm sure he doesn't want us to curse."

The producer laughs nervously. The lights are hot and the Doctor's Wife feels sure she's perspiring. She takes her compact out of her purse and powders her forehead so she's not too shiny. She hopes it's obvious to the viewers that she's pregnant and not just overweight.

The whole things is only fifteen minutes, enough time to talk about bacteria levels, the immediate and long term costs of the bond issue, and how it will be spread out over fifteen years so nobody gets socked with a huge bill all at once. There is to be a special election on October 16, 1958 for the bond measure. The interest on the bonds will be paid from monthly service charges and the charges will be capped at $4.50 a month. The Doctor's Wife is satisfied that she has all of the facts in order in her head.

"Four, three, two," the cameraman says, counting down with his fingers. The cameras begin rolling. This is a live show.

"Everybody remembers a couple years back when the algae bloomed and it started to smell," the Doctor's Wife says.

"It was terrible," Nancy agrees.

The Doctor's Wife gives her speech. This seems to be going spectacularly well. A page of Frank's notes slips from the coffee table. Frank starts to talk. "350 people showed up to the first Community Development meeting—out of a town of 3,500!"

Nancy, smiling brightly at the camera, reaches for the coffee pot, starting to freshen up the cups. Frank moves his leg excitedly as he talks, crumpling the notepaper underneath his foot, but he doesn't notice the noise he makes. An assistant crawls on his hands and knees below the camera shot. Nancy pauses mid-pour as the assistant creeps toward them. The coffee keeps coming, overflowing the cup and streaming down the side of the table. The producer is gesturing frantically at the cameraman. The cameraman pans the camera up so that the spilling coffee won't be filmed.

"Nancy," hisses the Doctor's Wife.

Nancy jerks the coffee urn upright.

"Well, that went beautifully," the Doctor's Wife says afterward.

"Think they'll ask us back?"

"Not likely," the Doctor's wife says, but the children are excited. Chrissy wants to know if this means the family is moving to Hollywood.

Zoology

Ace howls, scratching frantically at the front door. Chrissy opens the door to see quills protruding from his muzzle. "Grandma!" she screams for Petie, visiting from Lawrence, Kansas. Petie grabs Chrissy by the shoulders and moves her. The screen door slams shut and Ace continues to howl.

"Bring me pliers from the workbench downstairs," Petie orders.

Chrissy flies down the basement. When she comes back upstairs, she helps her grandma turn the kitchen floor into an operating room, the lights blazing, the rheostat at the highest level. Ace's eyes look very sad but he is stoic as Petie grabs a quill with the pliers, pulling the quill all the way through Ace's lip, into his mouth and then out. "We have to do it this way because the quills are barbed," Petie explains, showing Chrissy the barb with the tip of the pliers.

"Is Ace going to die?" Chrissy asks.

"No," her grandmother says. "Petrea" is Chrissy's real first name. Chrissy's whole name is Petrea Christina Hagen. Chrissy likes to think that she's like her grandmother, and not just because of her name.

When the operation is done, Ace is allowed to sleep in a nest of blankets on the utility porch in front of the washing machine, and Petie makes cinnamon toast for everybody.

"Tell us about Uncle Jack and the skunk," Chrissy asks.

"One day when your Uncle Jack was a boy he found an orphaned baby skunk and decided he'd bring it home. He thought that since the skunk was young its glands wouldn't be developed."

"Did he get sprayed?"

"He came back covered with the smell of skunk."

"Did you give him a tomato bath?"

"We tried. The smell never really went away until his hair grew out."

"He really took a bath in tomato juice?"

"We used huge cans."

"Did he ever keep snakes in the basement?"

"One time I was having a luncheon and I noticed snakes on the valence in the dining room."

"What did you do?"

"I moved on to coffee and dessert as quickly as I could without being rude." Her grandmother fixes her with a stare. "You know all these stories."

"He's a professor of zoology?" Chrissy asks. She loves the word zoo.

"Your uncle loves animals, just like you."

"Just like me," Chrissy says.

Sandy Beach Drive

"Hey dear, Petie and I bought a house today!" the Doctor had said to her. She'd propped herself up in the hospital bed, newborn Chrissy at her breast.

"You did what?"

"It's on the lake," he'd said, sounding pleased with himself. At the time, she'd wondered if she was hearing properly. She'd wondered if giving birth had addled her brain and she was having a small hallucination.

"It was built by a Norwegian doctor," Petie added. Petie thinks the Doctor is the best man who ever lived. The Doctor's Wife thinks this too, naturally, and at the time, she hadn't really cared what the house looked like. All of a sudden she'd had three kids to take care of and so it didn't matter that she'd loved Cherry Acres, the place they'd rented from the Manning family. Cherry Acres sat at the top of the hill, five acres of orchards overlooking the lake. The Doctor's Wife is not a person who needs to live on the water. She prefers a long view.

Bond Issue II

The second time Nancy and the Doctor's Wife go on TV, they've prepared a formal speech. The Doctor's Wife wears a tweed suit. The children are once again thrilled, and it seems like the vote will pass with no trouble.

"I think we did it," the Doctor's Wife says to Nancy.

"You need to know how to yell and stomp your feet to get things done. We're good at that," Nancy says.

The day before the vote, a local businessman distributes flyers that distort how much people will have to pay, and the bond issue fails by sixty votes.

Birth

It is Thanksgiving of 1958. Petie and J.W., Ann's grandfather, are staying with them to help out. Petie cooks everything, the turkey, the stuffing, two kinds of pies. But Ann is too excited to eat.

"You have a little brother," the Doctor says when he comes home from the hospital.

"What's his name?"

"John."

Ann is the first kid to hold him. His eyes are closed like a little puppy's. Chrissy hovers nearby, but Ann doesn't want to give him up.

Take Your Son

The first time the Doctor takes Bob fishing he makes a big breakfast of oatmeal, bacon, scrambled eggs, and toast. It's four-thirty in the morning and they need to get to the Skykomish as dawn breaks. If they're not there at the right time the fishing will be ruined. It can't be too dark, not too bright, not too cold, not too windy, but this seems like a perfect sort of morning, gray skies, calm.

The Doctor usually fishes alone. He has a few fishing buddies, but he wouldn't tell his best friend about a good steelhead run. The thing he likes about fishing is the solitude. He likes going into a sort of concentrated trance in which problems get worked out by being placed to the side.

Bob stays silent in the car as they drive past the tall firs that line the country road. The Doctor pulls off the side of the road in front of a gate on which a "No Trespassing" sign is posted. He helps Bob climb the gate. They walk down a dirt road alongside a pasture where cows stand still in the early morning mist, and then through a copse of poplars to where the cold river runs. The dark skies make the water look black as it flows around a giant granite boulder in the middle of the river.

Bob is wearing rubber rain boots since the Doctor doesn't own waders small enough for him. They've practiced in the front yard, casting out onto the lawn. Today Bob is not going to cast, he is to be quiet and he is to watch.

"Don't go in too deep. No noise."

Bob nods in assent.

The Doctor wades out. He casts as the world wakes, falling into a rhythm as the edges of the sky brighten. He hears a splash and he turns around to see Bob has fallen in the water.

"Swim, goddamn it!" the Doctor yells.

Table Manners

It wasn't Chrissy's fault last week when she knocked the dish of beets to the floor. And the week before she wouldn't have chewed with her mouth open, except she'd needed to say something when she'd just taken a bite. The week before that, it was true, in an attempt to make Ann sick, she'd mixed everything on her plate together, taking big bites of the mush. But this week Chrissy has been perfect.

The Doctor stands up. He clears his throat and Chrissy sits on the edge of her chair, looking up at him. The Doctor's manner is mock-formal, a pretend version of when he's in his office and you aren't allowed to joke around with him: "Welcome once again to the awards ceremony for this week's table manners prize. As you all know, the prize is awarded to the Hagen child who best behaves himself for the week. You may be disqualified for spilling milk, causing a fuss with one of your siblings, or leaving the table without being excused. A child receives extra points for not gobbling, for saying please, for passing food to the right, and for helping his mother clear the dishes."

Chrissy wishes that he would get to the prize-giving right away. The prize is always a pharmaceutical representative freebee: a little flashlight, a pen shaped like a syringe, an address book. This week it's a golden ruler. It's shiny and though it probably isn't real gold, it would be very easy to pretend that it is. Bob let out a very large burp earlier in the week right after they sat down for dinner and instead of saying excuse me, he followed it up with an even louder one. The sides of her mother's mouth had twitched, but her dad was not amused, and by the time Bob tried to say "excuse me," it was far too late.

Ann had to be told to take her elbows off the table two nights in a row, and she hasn't been a member of the clean plate club even once this week. John is three months old and he doesn't care about prizes, which is fortunate for him. He has atrocious manners.

Chrissy, in contrast to her slovenly, ill-bred siblings, has been a model citizen.

"This week I am pleased to announce the winner is—"

"Me, I won!" Chrissy blurts out. She is warm all over, blushing with pride in herself, and gleeful. Ann will be so disappointed.

"Chrissy."

Chrissy stands up and executes a passable curtsey as her dad bestows the golden ruler on her.

The Sunshine Club

The neighbor girls, Gail and Sue Berg, live across the street from the lake, so they don't have a dock and they don't much like swimming. Ann and Chrissy swim for the whole morning and early afternoon, but in the late afternoon, they meet the Bergs under the apple trees in the back yard for the daily meeting of the Sunshine Club. The Bergs and the Hagens are the founding members. Membership is closed.

Ann carries the Monopoly game and Chrissy holds the golden ruler. It's late August, and summer is almost over. The willow next to the road sways, and sunlight splashes down through the apple tree canopy. Ann reaches up to pick a not quite ripe apple. The Bergs think the apples are disgusting, that the little Gravensteins are too sour. This is another way in which the Hagens and the Bergs differ. Clubs are for people who are alike in some way and one way they are alike is that they love Monopoly.

Chrissy uses her ruler to draw a line beneath the final score of the last game. On Saturday, the Doctor's Wife made them cut their game short so they could come inside to listen to the broadcast of the Metropolitan Opera. Ann wanted to refuse, but unlike the Hagen children, the Bergs wouldn't dream of disobeying the Doctor's Wife.

The Bergs also got cookies from the cookie jar when they were done listening, as many as they wanted.

The Bergs have an older half-sister named Peralee who was named after her father Perry. Peralee has all of Elvis Presley's records and she knows every single word of the lyrics. Once she came and taught the girls how to hula dance underneath the apple trees. Usually she is too old and important to come. None of the Bergs came yesterday, Sunday. The Bergs are religious in a way that the Hagens aren't. They have to go to church twice, in the morning and in the evening, which leaves no time for the Sunshine Club.

Ann passes out the money at the beginning of the game, two $500 bills, two $100 bills, and so on. You have to watch Chrissy with the money. She has been known to tuck an extra hundred or two in her shorts pocket. Chrissy sits on the golden ruler so nobody else can touch it.

Ann is the little dog. She rolls the dice, settling in to the game. It's hard to imagine doing anything else other than the routine of swim, lunch, swim, Sunshine Club, dinner, bed. It's hard to imagine school ever starting again.

John

John is a smart baby. One day when the family is driving down to Seattle, Ann and Chrissy teach John to say "pee yu" and plug his nose. John giggles, as do the girls; Bob, the Doctor and the Doctor's Wife all laugh too. It is not every eleven-month-old baby who could learn how to do that.

The Bone Table

John is a year-and-a-half and he's not walking, so the Doctor's Wife takes him to the pediatrician.

"Your son is retarded," the pediatrician says.

"No," the Doctor's Wife says, "No, I don't think that's it." She picks up John, walking out of the office, past the receptionist who she knows but does not acknowledge on the way out, even though when they were waiting, the receptionist came out from behind her desk to bring John a lollipop. This is rude, but she's mad. She'll get a second opinion. Or a third.

Driving in a light drizzle, the Doctor's Wife takes John to the grocery store. They make their way to the butcher counter.

"I want hot dog," John says.

If he were retarded, he couldn't talk, at least not like this. John is more verbal than her other kids at the same age and those kids aren't half dumb. Hot dogs. The Doctor's Wife doesn't care for them, but if the kids have them, she and the Doctor can eat liver and onions, which the kids refuse to touch and make gagging noises over. Pat Dussler is working. "Give me a pound of liver and ten hot dogs."

"Does somebody want his own hot dog for the road?" John grins at Pat as he reaches for the hot dog.

Later that evening, the Doctor's Wife soaks the liver in milk. She's made coleslaw to go with the hot dogs. The girls play in the living room, taking care of John. She pokes her head in. "How's John doing?"

"He's not sick," Ann says.

"What do you mean?" The Doctor's Wife is curious and irritated.

"I felt his forehead and he's not hot at all. Why did he have to go to the doctor?"

"I listened to his heartbeat," Chrissy says, brandishing the Doctor's old stethoscope, the broken one mended with surgical tape.

Now the kids, including John, stare at her. They want her gone. The door swings shut behind her. She slices onions. This is a very simple dinner, but she still likes to get everything done in advance. At the last minute she'll fry the onions, flour the liver and fry it in the same pan. The salad can be made ahead of time. The Doctor should be home soon and then they can talk. There is a sharp sound of glass breaking.

"What's going on?" the Doctor's Wife asks, pushing the swinging door into the living room.

"I didn't do anything. It just fell over on the bone table," Chrissy says. The bone table is the name the kids have given a big, round, low, coffee table made of porous marble. It does look like bone, ossified, and on the table there is a broken glass vase. Tulips are strewn across the surface.

"Nobody move," the Doctor's Wife says.

"She's the one who broke it," Ann says.

The Doctor's Wife doesn't care who broke the vase. She just wants it cleaned up. The rest of the living room is a disaster. The girls have dragged out their dolls, undressing them. John gives her a wide-eyed look up from his Taylor Tot, a blue scooty thing with four little wheels that he can push himself around on.

The Doctor's Wife slouches down to pick up a doll on the way out of the living room. She'll have to clean up the glass herself if she doesn't want anybody to get cut. If one of the kids is hurt, she'll have to load everybody in the car and drive them to the Doctor's office where they'll have to wait and everybody will get hungry and cranky.

"Stay right where you are," the Doctor's Wife says again, going into the broom closet for the vacuum cleaner and a rag. The pieces of glass are quickly sucked up. "You finish," she says sharply to Chrissy. Chrissy takes the hose with a dramatic sigh and pushes the vacuum cleaner across the floor.

"Ann, you can tidy and dust."

"It's going to smell when you cook the liver, isn't it?" Ann asks.

"That's why you are having hot dogs."

"Yuck!" both girls say.

"I don't know who is going to win the table manners prize this week with that kind of behavior."

At dinner, the Doctor's Wife thinks: John can sit up. Sitting up isn't a problem. Chrissy has cut up her hot dog and is stirring it in to her coleslaw to make a vile mess. The Doctor's Wife doesn't have the energy to scold.

"Best liver I ever had," the Doctor says. They'll talk when they go to bed, he says with his eyes. But what will they say? How will talking make whatever is wrong better? She touches John's hand, but he doesn't want to be fussed over. He thinks he's fine too. Maybe he is. The Doctor's Wife has made an apple pie for dessert. The house is clean and the kids are fed.

Dogfight

Ace and Rookie, a German Shepherd who lives on the other end of the road, have Sandy Beach Drive divided up between them. They meet in the center, teeth bared, every now and then. That's what's happening now. Chrissy is with Bob. Bob and Cathy Gunderson, the owner of Rookie, are fighting about who has a better dog.

"He had porcupine quills in his muzzle, and he didn't even complain when my grandma pulled them out," Bob says.

"Rookie wouldn't be that stupid."

"Ace is way smarter than Rookie," says Bob, snorting.

"Prove it."

"You prove it," says Chrissy.

The older kids ignore her. Anyway, this is to be a battle of brawn instead of brains. The dogs stare at each other, the fur on their necks bristling. A low growl comes from Ace's throat. Chrissy can feel her own neck hairs rise. Then she hears her mother calling them back for dinner.

When Chrissy and Bob run home, Ace follows.

Ann is seated on the couch with John, holding him as he tries to squirm away.

"There was almost a dog fight," Chrissy says.

"Set the table," her mother says.

"Rookie is a bad dog."

"Forks on the other side."

Chrissy knows how to set the table and she doesn't like being told. The fork goes on the left side with its partner the napkin and on the right side the knife protects the spoon from the fork. The knife is Ace and the fork is Rookie. They growl at each other.

"Don't put your fingers all over the silverware," her mother says.

Chrissy is not allowed to do a single thing.

Dinner is to be pork chops, baked potatoes and wilted salad. Chrissy is interested in the preparation of the dish, or rather the difference between the name of the dish and the way that it tastes. Her mother takes hot bacon grease and pours it on the salad with a dash of vinegar.

At dinner Chrissy chops up her pork chop into small pieces. She scoops the white stuff out of the brown potato skin and then takes her fork to mix everything together until it looks like it's already been chewed. She does this for two reasons. One, it tastes good. Two, it drives Ann crazy. Chrissy draws the jumble into her mouth. Nobody notices because John has made a mush of his own food and smeared it all over his face. Ann doesn't think that's gross. She thinks its funny.

"Don't you like the jacket of the potato?" her mother asks. "That's where the vitamins are."

Chrissy doesn't think this deserves a response. She drinks her milk, watching as Ace curls himself up on the back porch. "We should get another dog."

"The last thing we need is another dog."

"Dad, we should get another dog. I think Ace and Gretel are lonely."

"Hmm," he says, but Chrissy can tell that he likes the idea. He loves dogs as much as she does.

No

One day, the Doctor's Wife comes home to find stickers on each phone that read, "No."

"What are these for?" she asks the Doctor.

"I want you to learn to say no to people."

The Doctor's Wife doesn't think her husband has any idea how things work.

The Nurse Doll

The Doctor's Wife is distracted. She sits at the kitchen table, smoking. John is finally asleep. His brain is still sharp but his motor skills are regressing. Ann is trying to ask her something.

She stubs out her cigarette. "What?"

"Am I going to get a nurse doll tomorrow?"

It's Christmas Eve and for two months preceding the Doctor's Wife has heard just one thing out of Ann's mouth. "I thought you wanted a wedding doll," she says.

"No." Ann shakes her head. "I always only wanted a nurse doll."

Once the older kids are in bed, the Doctor's Wife undresses the doll. It's about a foot tall. Its face is made of bisque. The doll wears white shoes painted on her feet. Those will do. She holds the wedding dress up and looks at it critically, unsure whether she needs to take it apart at the seams to make a pattern.

The model she has in mind is Clara Barton. She takes down an old sheet from the linen closet then sets up the ironing board in the sewing room, clicking on the iron to heat. She'll starch the sheet stiff and then cut it up to make the uniform and hat. The hat will be tricky. The Doctor's Wife is not what she would call artistic. She has some navy blue wool for the cape and some red satin scraps to line the cape with.

At midnight, the Doctor's Wife looks up to see her husband at the door to the sewing room. "Come to bed. She doesn't need a nurse doll."

But you do what you can.

"She's very spoiled," is all the Doctor's Wife can think to say.

Bedtime

Chrissy has to have the bedroom door open and the hallway light on because she's afraid of the dark. "I can't sleep with the light off," she explains to Ann, who by now should know that this is true and yet is still angrily flouncing around in her bed. "Just put the pillow over your head."

"I get hot and I can still feel the light on my arm."

"No you can't."

"I have a math test tomorrow," Ann says.

Chrissy can see the justice in this and would like to be generous, but Ann does sleep at night and Chrissy wouldn't sleep at all if the light is turned off. She's tried. Even when the hall light is on she can convince herself that there's a shape in the shadow in the corner. If she fixes her eyes on the shape, it moves, and the movement proves there's something hunched there. Hunched!

Chrissy climbs out of bed, checking the corner where she saw the figure. There's nothing there. She shuts the closet door. It's not clear whether it is better to keep the door open or closed. If it is open you can see inside. If it is closed you can worry about what the door is hiding. Chrissy looks over at Ann. She lies artificially still, her arms rigid against her sides and her eyes screwed shut.

"You're not sleeping," Chrissy says. She goes over and repeats in Ann's ear, "You're not sleeping."

Ann leaps up. "You're dead," she says. Chrissy runs out of the room. Ann isn't violent, but she's mean. She'll say something about the gap between Chrissy's front teeth, she'll make her feel stupid, or she'll chant "Chrissy Wissy, she drinks whiskey."

"What's going on upstairs?" the Doctor's Wife calls.

"Nothing," Chrissy yells back down, hoping that Ann won't contradict her. But Ann apparently only meant to chase her out of the room. What is Bob up to? Chrissy sneaks past John's room, keeping her back against the wall like a spy until she can press her eye against the crack in the space between the wall and the edge of the door. Bob has his taxidermy kit out. There are dangerous tools involved—big needles and knives—and Chrissy isn't allowed near the kit. But neither is Bob allowed to have it in his bedroom. It should be down in the basement with the muskrat skins.

"You're not supposed to have that," she says, strolling into his room. There's no need to be surreptitious when Bob is breaking the law.

"Scat rabbit!"

"I'm going to tell." She sits herself down on the edge of his bed.

Bob is quick. He doesn't hit, he never hits, but he picks her up, pinning her arms to her side and then throws her on his bed.

Chrissy screams. "I'm going to tell! You have dangerous tools in your bedroom!"

The Doctor's Wife comes upstairs. "Everybody is going to sleep. Right. Now."

It's only then that Chrissy notices that Ann has heartlessly turned off the hall lights.

"Will you turn the light back on?" Chrissy asks her mother.

Click. Ann sighs. Chrissy looks in the corners again. It isn't a monster she's afraid of.

It's the *something* in the dark that's scary.

Easter

Ann and Chrissy wear matching dresses that the Doctor's Wife made, navy blue and white checked cotton, white gloves, white hats, and brand new patent leather shoes. They sit in a pew at the Congregational Church in Everett even though everybody else in the whole world goes to Ebenezer Lutheran in Lake Stevens. Ann is waiting for Chrissy to do something bad to break up the tedium of the service. Chrissy has started to pull at a little string and make a run in her stockings, which is promising.

Bob looks stunned, his hair is slicked back, and his face is kind of pimply. Ann would like to make fun of him, but he looks so uncomfortable stuffed into his new suit, which somehow already appears small in the leg, arm, and trunk. With one hand, the Doctor's Wife tugs at the suit jacket. With her other arm, she holds on to John. Ann is worried that she is going to be adjusted too, so she scoots away from her mother, closer to Chrissy.

Ann's tights are bunched at her knees and she picks at the wrinkle, causing her mother to hiss, "Stop that," which isn't fair at all since Chrissy has now pulled the run all the way down to her ankle. Finished with her stocking, Chrissy now has her hands folded in front of her chest and she crosses her eyes. She's trying to make Ann laugh, but Ann refuses. The face works on John, who shrieks with delight. The Doctor's Wife gets up abruptly to take him outside. Ann wishes she could go outside too. The minister drones on. It's dark gray outside and over the noise of the sermon Ann can hear rain dumping on the roof. Chrissy tries again, rolling her tongue into a tube shape, quietly humming "Oh What a Beautiful Morning," through her tongue like a kazoo.

John hangs on to her mother's neck as they ease back into the pew. Ann would like to be held too, so she scoots closer to the Doctor's Wife. John blinks down at her and, without thinking it seems, the Doctor's Wife puts him down on Ann's lap. Ann is going to turn eleven in July. She's ten now, practically a grownup, very unlike Chrissy.

After church they have to go to the country club for the Easter egg hunt. Bob has won the past Easters, so this year he's been barred from entering. Ann preferred it when her parents organized Easter egg hunts at home. The Doctor's Wife would usually write a poem for Ann and the others to read as they searched, the poem giving clues to where the eggs were hidden. For the country club hunt all you have to use is your eyes. The rain has petered out and now the weather is just raw.

The girls take turns carrying John, searching for eggs with him. "I see," he says, pointing, causing the girls to gallop down the hill toward a stand of pine trees.

"Here," Ann says, putting his feet on the ground. "You can get it yourself."

He makes a fat fist around her finger, unsteady on his legs. She lets go of him and he collapses on the muddy ground. He drags himself to a pine tree and tries unsuccessfully to hitch himself up, grunting with the effort.

1960

Dear Petie and JW,

Just a quick note about John. We took him to Seattle last Wednesday, May 25 and spent all morning at a pediatrician's and all afternoon at the neurologist.

Your daughter typed a rough copy of the neurologists reports to the other doctor, which is enclosed. John had about the most complete exam by both of them that you could have imagined. Probing, pinching, blood tests, x-rays, even an electro-encephalographic study.

Their conclusion is that everything is normal and that he just doesn't walk yet. They think everything will be all right. We feel better and are hoping every day now. He gets around in his Taylor Tot much better already and we bought him a scooter. He is just as sweet as ever and cuter as you will see this summer. He has a squint in the left eye, which we are going to take him to an eye specialist about this summer.

We would like you to come anytime. We will be gone for two weeks approximately, to take the kids to California. John will stay at home.

I'm going to fly to Miami June 12 and return June 19 to the AMA convention. Will see my brother and family there.

Write Soon,
RFH

Broken Bones

They feel it's important not to deprive the older kids of trips to educational places, so they've left John behind with Hazel Adelsheim while they take the rest of the kids to San Francisco. A lady is still expected to wear white gloves in San Francisco and the Doctor's Wife is also wearing heels, high but not spiky, and a new hat. She's meeting the rest of the family in Union Square after an unsuccessful trip to I. Magnin. It's nearly impossible to find a dress that looks remotely attractive.

While crossing Powell Street, the heel of her right shoe wedges in the trolley track, and down she goes, breaking her fall with her hands.

"I hurt my arm," the Doctor's Wife tells her husband when she meets up with him and the kids.

He takes a look at it, grunting. "Well, let's go get something to eat."

"But I hurt my arm."

"The kids are hungry."

"Yes, dear," the Doctor's Wife says ironically.

In a way, the Doctor is right, it'll take a long time to be attended to in the emergency room and the kids will get cranky if they haven't eaten. This is the Doctor's way of thinking: that you have to take care of everybody else's bodily desires before you treat the wounded. Nevertheless, the Doctor's Wife's arm throbs and she feels extremely queasy.

They take a taxi to a restaurant. "This place looks fine," the Doctor says, running his eyes over the silverware set on the tables. They get a booth. The Doctor's Wife is not hungry even a bit, but she orders broiled Petrale sole. The kids order fish and chips. The Doctor orders the Captain's plate, and when the food comes, nobody eats but the Doctor.

Home

On Sunday afternoons, it's Ann's job to rub John's back. He lies on the couch, his fists closed tight and limbs stiff. John has trouble breathing. He can't talk and he's going blind.

What's it like to go blind? The squint in his right eye is worse. That eye barely opens and the other one doesn't seem to be able to make out when Ann or Chrissy make a funny face.

While Ann rubs, Chrissy puts LPs on the record player, a large piece of furniture that has speakers integrated into the cabinet. Chrissy presses a button and the record drops down, the needle hits.

"Pianissimo, girls," the Doctor's Wife says, poking her head in from the kitchen.

Ann wishes her mother would just leave them alone. John doesn't mind the music. His head turns to follow her around and she thinks that he would smile if he could. These are good songs. The girls listen to musicals: *South Pacific*, *Camelot*, *Oklahoma*. *The Sound of Music* plays now. Ann has memorized all the words, and so has Chrissy. They sing along, but not too loudly. Ann continues to pat as she's been instructed.

School

Cathy Gunderson runs up the steps just as the bus gets ready to pull away form the Sandy Beach Drive stop. Cathy's coat is unbuttoned and her hair uncombed. Ann and Sue Berg share significant looks and then wait until Cathy has passed before they start talking again.

"It's too bad for her," Sue whispers.

The best part of school this year is that the fifth graders of Lake Stevens get to go to their very own school house, a little clapboard-covered building. Pioneer times are Ann's favorite part of Washington State history, and she's glad she gets to study pioneers in a real old schoolhouse that probably had pioneers as students. Mrs. Zuckerman has even promised to make hasty pudding for the class. Ann is wearing an itchy wool dress and ugly saddle shoes, but she imagines herself in cool calico and lace-up boots.

Glenwood School has an old bell that each student gets to pull in turn. Sue has already had a chance to pull the bell, but that's because her last name starts with B. Hagen comes after Gunderson. Cathy Gunderson was supposed to ring the bell first, but she got caught chewing gum. Mrs. Zuckerman made her go spit it out in the trash can in front of the whole class, and then Mrs. Zuckerman said that Cathy would have to move to the end of the bell ringing list, which means Ann's up next. It's a bit of a scandal.

"The bell is pretty heavy, so you have to put your weight into it," Sue whispers with the authority of experience. Ann doesn't need Sue to tell her what it'll be like. She can imagine exactly how it will feel, her hands closing around the thick, rough rope, the way she'll brace her legs against the floorboards and lean her torso back.

The bus twists its way around the lake along the Davies Road. After it crosses the bridge over the creek, it turns up the hill and pulls in front of the school. Glenwood School has only three rooms, two classrooms and a room with a stage in it that's used as a cafeteria and auditorium. When it rains—and it rains a lot—the kids stay inside the room with the stage for lunch and recess. They aren't allowed to run around like they normally do. They have to participate in planned activities, like dancing. Mrs. Zuckerman has taught them the hora and how to square dance. According to Mrs. Zuckerman, everybody needs to know how to dance, but Ann isn't so sure about that.

Today after lunch—rain, but bingo instead of dancing—they return to the classroom to sit and listen to the Standard School Broadcast. A pianist plays a very difficult sounding Rachmaninoff piece. Ann would like to play Rachmaninoff someday. She taps her fingers on her desk like it's a keyboard, pretending that her left hand is making the big chords and her right is carrying the melody. Sometimes she has to be forced to practice the piano by her mother instead of going right to the piano herself every day, but that doesn't mean she doesn't also love playing. A few of the other kids in the class are yawning. Sue Berg is busy drawing a dog and Jimmy Halverson has put his head down on the desk. He'd better not let Mrs. Zuckerman catch him doing that.

The Standard School Broadcast ends and it's time for Washington State history. The class starts a unit about Marcus and Narcissa Whitman. Mrs. Zuckerman tells the class to silently read the chapter. Ann likes the reading-to-herself part of the school day the best. The gist of the history chapter is that the Whitmans traveled west in 1836, settling in Walla Walla so that they could convert the Indians to Christianity. In 1847 the Whitmans and the other missionaries were massacred by the natives they were trying to convert. Ann is fairly positive that the word massacred means that the Whitmans were scalped. Her head pricks at the idea of cold metal slicing skin from skull. This is not how she likes to picture pioneer life, and she shuts the history book with distaste.

She scans the room. Mrs. Zuckerman is writing questions on the board, Sue is reading, frowning, and Jimmy is folding a paper airplane. When she looks to the back of the room, her eyes lock with Cathy Gunderson, who has apparently been glaring at her. Ann feels herself start to blush. She faces the front of the room, still feeling Cathy's look burning into the back of her head. It wasn't Ann's fault that Cathy chewed gum and got in trouble for it. But Ann doesn't like to feel as though she's hurt anybody's feelings.

Next, it's time for Language Arts. Mrs. Zuckerman makes an announcement that during the month of October there will be a competition to see who can memorize the most poems. "To receive points you need to recite the poem in front of the class exactly as it is printed on the page."

"What do you get if you win?" asks Sue Berg.

"The person who wins will be the valedictorian." There is a blank silence. "Does anybody know what a valedictorian is?" Mrs. Zuckerman asks. No, nobody does. Ann thinks it sounds medical.

"A valedictorian is the person who has the highest grade in the class—usually the word refers to the person in high school or college who has the best grades. I was making a joke just now," Mrs. Zuckerman says.

This is a poor sort of a joke if it is a joke at all, and nobody laughs. Ann has the highest grades in her class now, and in eighth grade, when high school starts and there are periods with different teachers, she'll make sure she gets the highest grades in all of those classes too. It doesn't sound that difficult to her. All it takes is hard work and she is good at that. So it's settled, she will be the valedictorian of both the poem memorizing contest and of her high school.

"How long does the poem have to be?" Sue Berg asks.

"At least fifteen lines."

Jimmy Halverson groans. This will be easier than Ann thought.

"Do we have to do it?" Jimmy Halverson asks.

"No."

Right before the end of the school day, Mrs. Zuckerman says, "Ann please remember that you are ringing the bell tomorrow." Of course Ann remembers.

On the way to the bus, Cathy Gunderson yanks Ann's hair at the back of her head. "Hey you."

"What?" Ann asks.

"I hope you know you have blackheads on your nose."

"So," Ann snaps back. But she is shocked. She blinks quickly and her chin wobbles, but she is not going to show any sort of emotion.

"You don't either have blackheads. She's just jealous," Sue whispers to her, looking behind at Cathy.

Ann knows she's been insulted, and she'd like to talk to Sue about the blackheads, but she's embarrassed. She doesn't actually know what blackheads are. At home, Ann examines her nose in the mirror of the downstairs bathroom. Cathy is right, there are little specks of black on the tip of her nose. Those must be the blackheads. Is it dirt? Is it a disease? What's going to happen to Ann now? Will they spread? Ann feels the tears come. The only benefit of crying is that it blurs her vision and she can't see her disgusting nose. Ann hates Cathy and wishes she would trip and break her wrist or that a dog would bite her or that her hair would fall out in clumps.

"Ann's crying," Chrissy sings when Ann opens the bathroom door.

"What's wrong?" the Doctor's Wife asks, stubbing out her cigarette in an ashtray. She immediately rinses the ashtray under the tap, cranking closed the window over the sink.

"Cathy Gunderson said I had blackheads."

"What's a blackhead?" Chrissy asks.

"A blackhead is a clogged pore," the Doctor's Wife says. "Let me see."

She takes Ann's face in her hands. Now Ann feels worse. She doesn't care to be examined this closely. The Doctor's Wife squints and Ann has a sudden quick horror about what she is going to be forced to do. The usual treatment for any sort of ailment—a splinter, a cut, a hangnail, an ingrown hair—is to soak the offending appendage in a bowl of salty water made as hot as you can stand it. Ann imagines dipping her nose in that. No thank you.

"Scrub it with a warm, soapy washcloth," the Doctor's Wife says, dropping Ann's jaw, turning around to go up the stairs. Ann follows her mother into John's bedroom. Scrubbing isn't so bad. "How are you feeling darling?" the Doctor's Wife asks John, running her hand over his forehead, behind his neck, checking his diaper in one movement.

Doesn't she know John can't answer? "I need to memorize a poem."

"What poem?"

"It has to be at least fifteen lines."

"Can it be part of a poem?"

"I guess so," Ann says. She hadn't thought about that.

"What about Walt Whitman?" the Doctor's Wife asks. She quickly changes John's diaper, his clothes, fluffs his pillow, kisses him on the forehead. She doesn't say anything to Ann while she's doing this.

"Who's Walt Whitman?"

"Look him up."

"Will you help me practice?"

"What?"

"Practice my poem."

"Hurry downstairs. Look on the bookshelf in the living room. Go scrub your face and find your poem."

"Then will you help me?"

"Get your sister to help." Chrissy is going to be worse than useless at this. As Ann takes the stairs one at a time, she hears her mother reading a book to John. In the living room, Ann finds Walt Whitman. The whole book is a poem! What if she memorized the whole thing? Is that even possible? She looks at the cover, the name Whitman sinking in. What an odd coincidence. She wonders if Walt is related to Narcissa and Marcus. What if he was a cousin? Her cousins are in Florida and during one visit Ann got to eat Key lime pie made with real Key limes. The pie was tart and delicious and she wouldn't mind having a piece right now. She'd mention to her mom that she'd like to make some Key Lime pie, except that her mother has made it clear that she doesn't have time for anything extraneous.

The first part of the book is called "Song of Myself." She'll memorize the first twenty lines to make sure that she's done what she is supposed to. Surely she couldn't be expected to memorize the whole book, even if she could? Even if she wanted to? Twenty lines should be fine.

The only way to memorize anything is to practice it over and over. She lies down on the long couch in the living room and mouths the words to herself for hours before dinner. If you want to win the table manners prize you can't read during dinner. Ann skips dessert to run through the poem with her mother, both of them sitting blissfully alone in the living room. When she's in bed, she tries to fix the poem in her head before she sleeps.

"What I assume you shall assume," Ann whispers to herself again.

"Shut up," Chrissy says, holding a pillow over hear head. "I'm trying to sleep. Why do you have to whisper so loud?"

Ann has been kept awake her whole life by the hall light. Chrissy can shove it. Ann stops whispering and says the words in a normal voice. Chrissy leaps out of bed carrying her pillow with her and whacks Ann's book out of her hand, sending it flying across the room. Ann calmly gets out of bed and picks up the book from the floor, settling back into bed.

"Goodnight, girls," their mother says, poking her head in, which prevents Chrissy from retaliating immediately.

The next morning, Ann runs over the lines before breakfast. She'd like to double-check the lines on the bus, but it makes her carsick, and there isn't any time to really practice before school because she has to ring the bell. She doesn't even really enjoy ringing the bell because as she pulls the rope she thinks about the lines of the poem, repeating them to herself.

"Does anybody have a poem to recite today?" Mrs. Zuckerman asks after the Pledge of Allegiance.

Ann's shy, so she'd rather not get up in front of the class, but at the same time she has to win. She raises her hand.

"Ann? Anybody else?"

No, there's nobody else, and Mrs. Zuckerman calls Ann to the front of the classroom.

Ann takes a deep breath and focuses on the map of Washington State at the back of the room. The words—as they've been trained to do—march from her brain to her mouth, spoken as they were learned. When she's done, she stops.

"Perfect," Mrs. Zuckerman says. That's what Ann likes to hear.

Eggs

The Doctor's Wife can't get any protein down John. The solution she and her husband come across is to soft-boil eggs, barely cooked really, so that they can slip nourishment down his throat. He's wasting away because he doesn't have enough to eat. Anybody would go into decline if he couldn't eat.

Study Club

When the Doctor's study club comes over, the Doctor's Wife and the kids are supposed to be scarce while its members analyze cigars, Canadian Club, and poker around the kitchen table. John is up with the Doctor's Wife in the sewing room. The kids are in the basement, roller skating around the furnace. The phone rings and the Doctor's Wife goes into her bedroom to answer. "Dorothy O'Hara for you. It's about Ace."

"Killed one of your chickens?" he asks after he picks up the extension in the kitchen. "Why don't I give you a free house call?"

"Two chickens?"

"Two house calls?"

This has happened before, and more than once. Ace has even taught Gretel to kill chickens. Ace lopes into the yard holding the chicken by the neck. "Bad dog," the Doctor mutters. The Doctor's Wife, the study club, and the kids file outdoors behind him. The Doctor takes the chicken from Ace's mouth. He takes a stout rope and ties it around the chicken's neck and then ties it to Ace's collar, who tries to bite the chicken but can't reach it. A week later, the chicken rots off Ace's neck. Ace is cured of his taste for live chicken.

Seizures

"Go get help," the Doctor's Wife yells at Chrissy. The Doctor's Wife is holding John down on the couch while he thrashes.

Chrissy runs next door, jumping from the retaining wall down to the driveway of Franny and Marylin Rubatino's house. She bangs on the door.

"Come quick, it's John," she says, "He's having a seizure."

Franny runs after her. When they get back to the house, Chrissy can't watch. She runs upstairs and buries her face in her pillow.

Bond Issue III

People try to sell their houses and they can't. Who wants to buy a house with a bad septic tank? Who wants to buy a house fronting a dirty lake? Nobody wants to change until it hurts more to stay the same.

A Sense of Humor

The eggs can't be too tough, but neither can they run, the Doctor insists. On the one hand, the Doctor's Wife understands her husband's finickiness. She hates the rubbery white part of a boiled egg. Nevertheless, yesterday when the Doctor complained about how she'd prepared the eggs, she'd flown into a rage, stopping herself at the last second from throwing a plate on the floor. "You can make your own eggs," she'd snapped.

"I'd be glad to," he'd replied calmly, which didn't help her mood.

What she can and will do is set the table, heat the water in the teakettle and balance the raw eggs on the counter, so that the Doctor can boil them when he is ready. She even makes him toast, flinging it on a plate, scraping it with butter. She'd be better off if she could sit down for a second and have a cigarette, but for that she'll have to wait.

"Breakfast is ready," she shouts upstairs. Where are the kids? She stomps up. She can feel herself stomping. The girls are sleeping in their twin beds, the brand new ones they'd immediately carved their names into with the beheaded tips of bobby pins. "Wake up, darlings," she says, clapping her hands loudly. Chrissy's leg hangs out of the bed and Ann opens her eyes.

"I'm awake," Ann says, sitting bolt upright.

"Well, get up."

She goes into Bob's room. "Rise and shine, baby," she says, opening the door. He's sitting at his desk in his pajamas, his taxidermy kit in front of him. He's holding an open jar of fake eyes. "Wash your hands and come down for breakfast."

The Doctor's Wife takes towels from the upstairs bathroom to the utility porch downstairs, where she throws them in the washing machine. She hates to have any laundry left over from the day before. She goes back upstairs to check on John, who is still sleeping, breathing raggedly. She kisses him on his forehead and rubs his back.

Downstairs, she sees that the Doctor has had his breakfast, but left his toast. Why does she bother? She dumps the toast into the trash.

"What happened to breakfast?" the Doctor asks when he emerges from the downstairs bathroom. The Doctor's Wife sees the eggs on the counter, sees that she's cleared his plate before he even sat down to eat.

She whoops with laughter. The kids come down in a stampede.

"What's wrong, mom?" Ann asks, sleep in her eyes, but sounding alarmed. The Doctor shakes his head.

Nobody else seems to think that what she did is at all funny. She is the only one with a sense of humor.

There's Nothing Bad That Can't Get Worse

The Doctor's Wife takes John down to Seattle Children's Hospital where she stays with him for five days while yet more tests are run. On the third day, a Saturday, the Doctor drives the other kids from Lake Stevens. Healthy children are not allowed in the Children's Hospital, so the Doctor's Wife holds John up at the window while she waves at the others standing down below in the parking lot.

Children's Hospital can't say what's wrong, so a few weeks later the Doctor's Wife takes John to the University of Washington Hospital, and there the neurologists can't say exactly either, but they finally have an idea. Electrical charges move along neurons to control everything we do. John's body doesn't make myelin, the protein that acts as a protective sheath around the neurons, so the electrical signals from his brain can't travel fast enough, and the signal goes uselessly into the surrounding tissues. What this means, for example, is that the electrical command is lost in between John's brain and his throat and so he can't swallow. That's all the doctors can say.

"Neurologists either know what's wrong and can't do anything about it, or they don't know what's wrong and can't do anything about it," the Doctor says to his wife. The Doctor and the Doctor's

Wife face a choice. They can take John to The Mayo Clinic or the Johns Hopkins, turning their lives over to useless hope. Or they can take him home.

They take him home.

Sleepaway Camp

Ann packs her vinyl suitcase. She doesn't usually like to spend any time away from home and she especially doesn't see the point of going to Campfire Girl camp. There's a lake to swim in and activities like archery and sailing, but Ann doesn't like activities. She likes to read and she likes to swim. She has her own lake right in the front yard. But she wants to prove to herself that she can be brave. Also her mother has sewn Ann's name into all of her clothes, and it's too late to back out of it.

"I'm going to have the room all to myself," Chrissy says. Ann places her rolled up socks in her suitcase. "And I'm going to sleep in your bed."

"I don't care."

"I'm going to sleep in your bed in my bathing suit."

"So."

"I'm going to put an earwig in your bed and it's going to lay eggs."

Ann hates the thought of earwigs and Chrissy knows it, but she keeps her mouth shut.

"You're so mean!" Chrissy shrieks.

Their mother comes in to the room and hugs them close. "Oh, Ann. Chrissy." Their mother is crying and she squeezes them. Ann knows what happened.

"Am I still going to go to Campfire Girl camp?"

"No, darling."

The Doctor and the Doctor's Wife think that it is necessary for the kids to see John's body so that they don't think of death as an unnatural event. The kids file in. What do they do? Where do they look? Their little brother is skinny from not eating and his chest doesn't move.

The Pacific War

The Doctor has been trying not to worry so much. He's on a fishing trip with Gretel and Bobby, who's thirteen. They're on the northern fork of the Stilliguamish, fishing for steelhead, but not right this moment. It's too late in the morning to fish. The Doctor and his son are eating ham sandwiches, standing up. Gretel follows the Doctor's every movement: hand to mouth, hand resting slack by the waist, then up to the mouth again.

The Doctor takes a drink from his beer can. A sharp, hot pain sears his throat. He drops his beer can on the ground and says, "Jesus Christ," but doesn't yell. Gretel laps up the spilled beer as it seeps into the riverbank. He didn't yell, because he doesn't like to yell, but he wishes he did. You never expect a bee sting to hurt as much as it does.

"Bee stung my throat," the Doctor says by way of explanation to his son.

"Is the bee still in there?" asks Bob.

"I'm pretty sure I swallowed it," the Doctor says, surprised to think this is true.

"Where's the stinger?"

The Doctor harrumphs. "It seems to still be in my throat." If his throat starts to swell shut, something will have to be done quickly. He knows how to perform an emergency tracheotomy. The first he ever did was on the deck of the destroyer *O'Bannon*, off the coast of Guadalcanal. For the burned soldier shedding sheets of skin, the tracheotomy was as useless as the syrettes of morphine.

"If I pass out, I need you to help me," the Doctor says to his son. He takes a knife out of the tackle box, and a ballpoint pen from his shirt pocket, removing the ink reservoir from the pen's casing. He takes Bob's hand and guides his finger to the place between the Adam's apple and the cricoid cartilage. "With the knife, make a half-inch slit, pinch the cut, and then poke the tube through the hole. I'll regain consciousness when I can breathe again."

"OK," Bob says, drawing his hand to his own throat.

"Probably you won't have to do it," the Doctor says, handing his son the pen. Gretel, done with the beer, moves closer to the Doctor, putting her head under his right hand. "Good dog," the Doctor says.

"Dad?" Bob asks, coming close. Their hands almost touch on the top of the dog's head.

The Doctor looks at the river, birch trees leaning toward the water, the steelhead hiding in the shadows. Two big dragonflies buzz past, connected to each other, mating. Gretel, who might not be the smartest dog, lopes after the dragonflies, snapping her jaws.

"Dad?" Bob asks again.

"Yes?"

"What do I do after you wake up?"

PART II

Me

"When did you find out what John had?" I ask my grandmother on the telephone.

"We knew pretty soon after he died. We sent off tissue samples to Atlanta."

"To the CDC?"

"Yes."

"It seems like there aren't any journal articles about meta-chromatic leukodystrophy until the early sixties."

"That sounds about right."

We're quiet. The disease is still incurable. Nobody lives past the age of four.

"There are some things that are good to remember and some things that are hard to remember," the Doctor's Wife says.

Skis

On Christmas morning, six months after John's death, the Doctor's Wife directs the girls to the tree in the corner of the living room. Propped on a fir branch in front of a green light they find a small envelope with both of their names written on it. Chrissy is absolutely positive that the envelope was not there before today. She takes the envelope down. Inside she finds a typed poem, written by her mother and pasted on a card.

"Hooves" is rhymed with "moves." "Equine" is rhymed with "so don't you whine."

"What's equine?" asks Chrissy.

"Horses," Ann says.

Chrissy's heart beats fast. "We're getting horses!"

The girls are not, in fact, getting horses. But they get the second best thing, riding lessons at the Boggses Skyline Stables. The Boggses and the McLanes own B&M, the grocery store at Frontier Village, the new shopping center on the ridge above the lake. Taylor's Pharmacy, B&M and the rest of the buildings have false fronts meant to resemble those in an old western town.

The girls start the lessons in a wet, cold March, running home from the bus after school to change into jeans and sneakers. At the stables they learn things like, "The only person who doesn't fall off a horse is the one who doesn't get on." They learn how to ride Western, in which one leads with the reins, and how to ride English, in which one leads with the bit. When riding English, one posts when the horse trots, sitting up very tall in the saddle. While they take their lessons, Chrissy can't help but notice that her friend Alison Packer rides her own horse instead of a loaner. Rather than jeans and sneakers she wears jodhpurs, a little riding coat, and beautiful black glossy boots that come up past her knees.

"Who cares about that?" the Doctor's Wife says, when Chrissy asks for her own riding outfit.

"I'm going to save up and buy my own boots," Chrissy says to Ann when they're getting ready for bed.

"I have a better idea."

"How much do you think boots like that cost?" Chrissy says. She doesn't like Ann to have better ideas.

"Let's buy a horse," Ann says.

This *is* a better idea.

"How are you going to pay for a horse?" the Doctor's Wife asks the next day.

"We'll save our money."

"What money?"

She can scoff, but what else can she do? Nothing. It's their own allowance and they can do with it what they will. But by the time summer rolls around, it has become clear that saving up allowance money is not going to be enough. Fortunately, a solution presents itself. During strawberry season, an old white-painted school bus makes stops all along the road around the lake, picking up kids to take to the berry fields in Hamilton. Each strawberry flat earns the picker fifty cents.

The first day of the season, Chrissy and Ann wait for the bus with Cathy Gunderson and the Bergs, shivering in the gray morning. In the field the foreman teaches them how to do the job. The strawberries are meant for the cannery, so they have to be hulled, which means digging out the green stem with your fingers, and by the end of the day, Chrissy and Ann's hands are stained red. At home, the Doctor's Wife makes the girls dip their hands in a solution of water and Clorox until the red is gone.

Then Chrissy and Ann change into their bathing suits. The horse is important, but they wouldn't dream of having jobs if they had to work all day and couldn't swim.

One day after two weeks of picking, they are in the fields when an older kid hits Chrissy dead on the cheek with a hard little strawberry, compact as a stone. She pitches a strawberry back and then it's war.

"Over here," Chrissy yells, calling to her allies as she ducks behind a tractor. Cathy and the Bergs join forces with the Hagens against kids from the other side of the lake.

They see the foreman running across the field.

"Hey! You just cost me a hundred dollars," he yells. Chrissy feels slightly bad about this. She pulls strawberry chunks from her hair. "If you ever do that again you'll be sent home and the bus won't pick you up anymore."

If they get fired they won't be able to buy a horse!

"Take your clothes off outside," the Doctor's Wife says when they come home.

They've been continuously encouraged by their mother to open a savings account, but they don't think much of that idea. It is better to hold and count the money whenever they feel like it, so they keep their wages in a cigar box under Ann's bed. At the end of July, they shut the door to their room and spread the bills and coins out on Ann's bed.

"We have enough to buy a horse," Chrissy announces at dinner.

"Where will you keep it?" the Doctor asks.

"We can build a barn in the back yard."

"No, we can't," the Doctor says.

"We'll board the horse at the Boggses'."

"Do you know how much money it costs to board a horse?"

"It's not that much. Alison said her dad could get us a deal."

The Doctor's Wife laughs, a short, mirthless exhalation.

"We'll work at the stables and pay for the boarding ourselves."

"How will you decide who gets to ride the horse?"

"We'll trade off," Chrissy says firmly.

"Dad?" Ann asks.

"You're not going to buy a horse."

"Why not?"

"It isn't fair! We saved our own money!" Chrissy says, but they can't really complain that much since the riding lessons continue until the winter, when they discover the ski bus to Stevens Pass. On Sundays during January and February, the bus from Grammel's, the sporting goods store in Everett, picks them up at the end of the trestle and then continues on Highway 2 up to the mountains. If they go skiing they don't have to go to church, and there are boys on the bus.

The third Sunday they go, Chrissy has a new idea about how to spend their money. Once home, they take the cigar box out from under their bed to confirm they have enough to buy two pairs of snow skis.

"We aren't buying a horse," Chrissy says at dinner.

"Why not?"

"We're buying skis."

"Do what you want with your money," the Doctor's Wife says.

Memory

"She said what? I'm positive we didn't learn how to ride Western. We only learned how to ride English, I remember learning how to post," my mother says. "She's wrong about the snow skis too. We bought a water ski. I remember because it was really special, Roy Warnock at the marina made it."

"But you must not have been old enough to want a single ski. You didn't even have a boat then," I say.

"We didn't?"

Everybody remembers things differently. My mom remembers seeing John's body the day he died. But Chrissy, who since college has been known as Petrea, writes:

Mom called us in and told us John had died (plain words). His body was already upstairs, in the crib I think, that Mom and Dad put in the sewing area for him. I don't think I ever saw him (big mistake). Ann and I looked at each other and one of us said, "I didn't think I would feel so bad." Then we cried. The day after—or maybe the day or shortly after the funeral—we went on a picnic in some forest. And I thought how strange it was, and empty. I think now it was empty because we just walked out of the house and, for the first time in years, didn't leave John behind at home.

Petrea says to me on the phone, "Oh, and Bob and dad were hunting when dad got stung by the bee, not fishing. But I guess that's OK since these are like confabulated family stories."

I wrack my brain. What does "confabulated" mean? I look it up. To confabulate in the psychological sense is to make up stories to compensate for the loss of memory, which is correct in a way.

"What else do you remember?" I ask Petrea.

"Once, Mom and John were away at Children's Hospital for a couple of months. We'd go up on Saturdays and wave from the parking lot because healthy kids weren't allowed in the hospital."

"Months?" my grandmother asks. "No, I don't think so. One time we had to go up for a few days. It may have just felt like months. What I do remember is that we were supposed to have guests that weekend."

"Who were they?"

"Some friends of your grandfather. I didn't give a hoot what happened to them."

Outboard

He's trying as hard as she is. The Doctor hammers flattened pieces of tire to the pilings where the boat will rest. He wants the kids to have fun. He didn't have much of a childhood. When he was twelve, his father died of a heart attack. His mother died of grief a month later, then he and his twin brother were packed off to boarding school in Missouri. The Doctor's Wife understands this and she understands the kids have to be taught that life goes on whether you like it or not. But she also imagines her children being chewed up by the propeller of the boat.

"Come on in, Mom," the kids urge.

The Doctor's Wife steps in to the boat, a fast looking red and white thing propelled by a not-so-strong 75 horsepower Johnson outboard. She perches uneasily on the edge of the front seat. The dogs stand on the end of the dock barking wildly. Bob is to be the first water skier. He is a big boy, already taller than six feet. He has to hang on for a long time before he pops up out of the water. There are certain people on the lake who have powerful inboard boats, pretty mahogany Chris-Crafts, but the Doctor's Wife is not interested in having a particular boat. She is interested in living a productive life.

Boat Mechanic

"I got a job," Bob tells his mother after biking home from the marina. He takes cookies from Smiley, the ceramic pig cookie jar, and runs them under the water so that, for efficiency's sake, they turn into a mush he can shove in his mouth. He's bulking up for football.

"That's so gross," Chrissy says.

"What kind of a job?" the Doctor's Wife asks.

"Roy Warnock hired me to be a boat mechanic."

"You don't know how to fix motors. What did you tell Roy?"

"I told him I know how to fix outboards. I think I can learn," Bob says, cramming another wad of soggy cookies into his mouth. "Do we have any manuals?"

The Doctor's Wife retrieves the outboard handbooks from her boat file, one for the Evinrude used on the fishing boat, another for the ski boat. Bob takes them to his room.

A boat motor is fairly simple. Most outboards are two-stroke engines. The carburetor releases a fine spray of gasoline that mixes with the air in the chamber. Spark plugs ignite the mixture of gas and air. This explosion compresses the air, which leads to the movement of rotors and eventually the spinning of the propeller in the water. This much is clear to Bob already.

He reads the chapter on how to troubleshoot. You start with the ignition switch, examining it to make sure the key clicks in place. Next, you make sure that there isn't any corrosion and that the connections are made properly. If this is all functioning, you move on to inspecting the distributor. The distributor regulates the firing of the spark plugs by turning the rotor, touching the points of the lugs, which then connect to the spark plugs.

This is a bit harder than he thought it would be. He holds the image of the figure in his head as he goes down to the dock, manual in hand, and looks at the boat. He takes the cover off the motor, examining the pieces until they become fairly familiar.

The next day he bikes to the marina, taking with him a lunch packed by his mother, three sandwiches of buttered bread, ham, cheese and lettuce, a wax paper package of cookies, two apples.

Roy Warnock sets Bob to work. He seems to believe that Bob knows what he's doing.

Hurry Up

"Tell me about the time you slammed the car door on Mom's hand."

"I'd been trying all morning to get everybody out of the house. I finally got everybody in the car and ready to go and your mother started crying. I thought, 'What's that brat screaming about now?'"

"When was that? Was it when John was sick?"

"I don't know. I don't remember dates."

"Well what happened next?"

"She showed me her hand. Oh, I felt so guilty."

Halloween

The Doctor's Wife drapes a dyed black sheet around herself, cinching it at the waist. Looking in the downstairs bathroom mirror, she adjusts her warty green rubber mask. To finish off the look she places a white wig on her head, tying two long tendrils of hair under her chin. Confident the costume looks suitably scary, she pushes the mask to the top of her head, where it is held in place by the wig. She's worn the same outfit for the past couple of years, but this year, she's roped her mother in on the act. Petie is wearing a black dress and her long white hair, usually up, is brushed straight so that it falls to her waist. Petie is going to sit in the corner in view of the door and not do anything exactly but sit there and be creepy.

When the kids were younger, the Doctor's Wife threw a yearly party in the basement, leading their friends through the big door that leads from the outside. In the darkened interior, she set out bowls of skinned grapes meant to feel like eyeballs and noodles boiled to the consistency of brains. But the kids are too old for that now.

"Maybe nobody will come this year," the Doctor's Wife says.

"They'll come," Petie says.

The Doctor's Wife steps outside to make sure the porch looks right. The curtains in the kitchen are drawn and the Doctor's Wife has swapped the regular light bulb on the front porch for a blue light. She's draped spider webby stuff over the screen door and along the railings. A lit jack-o'-lantern sits on a small table next to the door.

"Come back inside, quick!" says Petie, who has been peering through a crack in the curtain. The Doctor's Wife hurries in, shutting the door behind herself. She adjusts her mask and takes up her noisemaker, the kind that when spun around makes a loud crackling noise.

There's a knock on the door. She throws the door open and jumps out on the porch, spinning the noisemaker. The children run screaming down the stairs, piling up at the bottom. One brave kid, a pirate, stops his retreat, forcing the others back upstairs, where the Doctor's Wife is waiting with a basket of candy. "I wasn't scared," says the pirate. But the Doctors Wife still has the mask on and the kid keeps looking in the corner, where Petie sits immobile.

"Yes! Yes! That was perfect," The Doctor's Wife says when they leave.

Petie gives her hair a quick brush.

Football

His senior year of high school, Bob is the center of the Lake Stevens High School football team. He likes certain parts of football, running, eating, lifting weights. He likes to push the sleds across the field. He likes the feeling of his feet digging into the ground and he doesn't even mind getting tackled. What he hates is to hit the other boys.

He's sitting in the locker room holding his helmet in his hands, working himself up to go out onto the field. It won't be long before the game is over. All he has to do is get on the field. All he has to do is block. He doesn't need to hurt anybody.

"You ready to go, big boy?"

"Yes, Coach," he says.

He runs out onto the field with the other players. The lights shine down brightly on the field. There's a big crowd for this game against Concrete High School.

Right before half time, the huge middle linebacker on the opposite side looks through his helmet into Bob's eyes. "I'm going to kill you," he says.

This isn't necessary at all.

The ball is snapped and Bob knocks the asshole flat on his back. He doesn't move. Bob helps him up. "Are you OK?"

The Concrete middle linebacker spits out blood and a tooth lands on the grass. "Get your hands off me."

After the game, a scout from the University of Washington is waiting. He claps his hand on Bob's shoulder. "I'd be very surprised if we didn't offer you a place on the U Dub team. What would you think about that?"

"I'd be honored, sir," he says, but he feels worried. In the locker room he strips his muddy clothes off. He can't imagine four more years of this. Bob is interested in something beyond what he's seen so far. He stands under the shower, aware of the other boys horsing around, celebrating the victory.

The Door to the River

My grandfather bought a five-acre piece of property on the Stilliguamish, meaning to use the land for fishing, but mostly we went for family picnics. The first time I remember going was when I was about two-and-a-half. I don't remember driving up past Arlington and then east, toward the mountains, through the long green valley. I don't remember my grandfather unlocking the gate or driving on the road to the edge of our property. I don't remember walking—maybe I was carried—through the thick stands of cottonwoods to our narrow strip of beach. I'm guessing my grandmother had made a lunch of fried chicken and bread and butter sandwiches. ("That's what you make for a picnic," she says, which may have been true once.)

All I remember is standing on a big mossy rock and then slipping into the cold river.

"You fell into the current and I thought, there goes my first son," my mom says when I ask her if I was actually in any danger. This seems awfully breezy, but my mother was younger then than I am now. John had died long before. There was no real reason to be superstitious, no reason to think that there might be an extra element of danger for the males of the family.

Broken Bones II

The Doctor likes to go to the Friday fish fry at the Everett Yacht Club. Chrissy has put on a fresh dress and brushed her hair, excited for the dinner out. The whole family is going even though Bob says he's broken his foot. The foot is likely just sprained and a trip to the emergency room will ruin everybody's evening, says the Doctor. Chrissy agrees.

Bob limps. His foot has been wrapped up and he uses crutches retrieved from the basement. Ann has brought a book, which Chrissy disapproves of. Colorful signal pennants swoop down from the ceiling in festive rows. The picture windows look out at the mouth of the Snohomish River, over Port Gardner Bay and in the distance, Whidbey Island. A band plays on a stage.

"Can we dance, Daddy?" Chrissy asks.

He takes her to the dance floor. She feels lucky to have her father to herself.

Remorse

Chrissy is sitting at the kitchen table, she has a huge zit on her face, and the doctor is holding her chin, looking down at her.

"It's a cyst," says the Doctor.

"What can you do about it?"

"I'll lance it." The Doctor already has his bag open.

"No," Chrissy shrieks.

"Do you want to get rid of it or not?"

"Yes, but I don't want—"

The doctor jabs her face. "Look at that pus roll out!" he says as he pulls the lancet from the cyst.

Chrissy feels woozy.

"Now it'll get better," he says.

Trying

"Hold on to the rope, Mom! Keep your legs together."

Her rotten children rev the engine of the motorboat. She's dragged halfway across the lake before she finally lets go. That's enough of that and nobody can say she didn't try, she thinks as she coughs up a couple hundred gallons of water.

The boat circles around, Bob at the wheel. Ann and Chrissy gather up the skis that have flown off her feet. They're laughing so hard they have to hold each other up.

"Let me in the boat."

"Try once more," they say, wheezing.

"Let me in right this instant."

"You almost have it. Try once more."

She puts on the skis and is again dragged through the water, again swallows half the lake. The scene repeats itself several more times. For the children, it is more hilarious each time.

Surf City

In the downstairs bathroom, Ann and Chrissy apply zinc oxide to their noses. It's the afternoon and they've both finished their jobs for the day. They are listening to KJR, hoping that either Jan and Dean or the Beach Boys will come on. The Doctor and the Doctor's Wife expect their children to be gainfully employed, so Ann has spent the morning in the Doctor's lab, scrubbing test tubes crusted with blood and other bodily fluids, while Chrissy babysat.

They've both already changed into the two-pieces that show their belly buttons. The Doctor's Wife is thankfully the sort of mother who understands that fashions change. Ann's is polka dotted. Chrissy's is red and white, bought at Frederick and Nelson and chosen because the colors match the boat. They snap off the radio, grab towels from the utility porch and pour themselves glasses of iced tea. Ann takes extra cut lemon out of the refrigerator. They go down to the basement where they collect the skis and life belts and then exit out the basement door to the side yard. They need more hands. Chrissy's towel slips out from under her arm and onto the lawn, and Ann drops the lemons in the sand, but they finally make it with all of their gear to the boat.

"Squeeze the lemon here," Chrissy says, indicating the top of her head. Both Ann and Chrissy are very blonde, but lemon intensifies the effect. Now they are ready to go. Ann turns the key. Chrissy uncoils the bow line from the cleat and then leaps into the boat as Ann steers the boat away from the dock, driving slowly until they're in the open water, where she pushes the throttle forward. It's the middle of the afternoon during the week, so there aren't many people on the lake. The sun catches the chop of the waves. A million flashes of light wink under the blue sky.

The first thing they do is pick Bob up from the marina. He fills the tank, they throw his bike in the boat, and then they drive to the middle of the lake where they turn off the motor and float.

Bob is going away to Stanford in the fall. He's not going to play football, and Ann is glad. She never liked the idea of her brother getting smacked around. He's really big, but that doesn't matter. Sometimes the littler guys go after the big one just to see if they can take him down. Ann stretches out on a towel on the floor of the boat so that the sun can go all the way into her bones. Chrissy dives over the side of the boat. She can be heard splashing in the water.

"Let's do something," Chrissy says when she climbs back in. She's dripping over Ann, which totally ruins the good the sun has done.

"What's wrong with lying here and tanning?"

"It's boring."

"You're boring."

"Let's torpedo," Bob says.

Torpedoing means that one person drives the boat as fast as it'll go and then the others dive off the side of the boat. The Doctor's Wife doesn't know about this game.

Bob volunteers to drive first. "Faster," Chrissy yells.

Ann perches on the side of the boat and then dives. The surface slaps her face and it's a stunning sort of concussion, then water up the nose and darkness. The depths of the lake call her down. There's a story that there's a train at the bottom of the lake, an accident from the days of logging.

But back up on the surface, the water sparkles, sunny, and Chrissy is bobbing next to Ann. They climb up the ladder at the back of the boat.

"My turn to drive," Chrissy says, grinning. There's no point in doing something fun just once.

In Contrast

"I was only depressed for, like, 40 years," Petrea says to me.
"Because of John?"
"Because of John."

The Body

The Doctor went to medical school with Tom Critchfield, a gynecologist who lives on the other side of the lake. He and Tom are still friends, and one evening at the end of a dinner party, the Doctor agrees to go waterskiing behind Tom's new boat.

The sun doesn't set until almost ten in the summer, but it's late, and as the sun dips below the trees, the sky turns orange. Smudges of gnats swarm just above the surface of the lake. Fish jump, plopping back into the dark water. A muskrat slips under the dock. The Doctor's Wife shivers, pulling her cardigan around herself. It should be time for a cigarette but she's just quit. She and the Doctor have always known smoking is dangerous, that it leads to death.

She and the others step down into the boat. The Doctor takes his shirt off and then jumps in the water, fastening the white life belt around his waist. The Doctor isn't like the kids. He can't be pulled up on one ski. He has to start on two and then drop one, so he sits in the water with the tips of the two skis poking above the surface. He gives the thumbs up signal and as the boat takes off, the Doctor's Wife feels herself pressed against the seat. She blinks her eyes against the rush of air. The Doctor rises, standing.

The Critchfield and Hagen kids cheer from the dock. Then something goes wrong. The Doctor's legs are wide apart, too wide. It's hard to make out his face. "Bring your legs closer together!" the Doctor's Wife shouts.

This doesn't work. His legs spread farther and farther and then when they can't possibly extend any more, he pitches forward into the water. Tom spins the boat around to pick up the Doctor as Vivian Critchfield coils the towrope. The Doctor's Wife doesn't know how to do that, nor does she care to.

"How are you, darling?" she asks as her husband climbs aboard the boat. She puts a towel around his shoulders.

He's pale. "I think I hurt my testicles."

"Har har har," Tom laughs.

This is the sort of thing Tom and the Doctor talked about at the dinner table when she and the Doctor were newlyweds in Seattle. They'd been so poor she lived in the Y and he lived at Swedish Hospital, saving until they had enough money to rent an apartment on First Hill. Every night they ate dinner in the hospital cafeteria. The Doctor and his friends talked about diarrhea, bowel movements. They talked about the gruesome things they'd soon see in the war. They talked about guts spilling out of bellies in the emergency room. The Doctor's Wife was certainly not reared that way. Her father was a professor, and neither he nor her mother would have put up with any discussion of bodily functions—not to mention malfunctions—at the dinner table.

When they get home she examines her husband. His scrotum is an angry purple.

"Do you want to put ice it?" she asks doubtfully.

"No need," he says. He's a conservative doctor, continuing to believe that the body can usually heal itself.

Lundeen's

During the day, Lundeen's is a private park. People pay to play on the beach and swim in the area between two big piers. When they were younger, Chrissy and Ann would walk to the end of Sandy Beach Drive and look across the creek at the people attending the annual Scott Paper company picnic and Chrissy would feel sorry for the people who had to work at the smelly pulp plant and only once a year got to come to the lake.

At night, the place turns into a roadhouse, and on weekend nights you can hear the bands playing. Once, the front seat of a car was found on the beach after a Saturday night. Lundeen's drives the Doctor's Wife crazy. All you have to do is mention it and she shakes her head, setting her jaw. This only makes Lundeen's more interesting for Chrissy.

One night that summer before Bob leaves for college, the Doctor and the Doctor's Wife are driving home from dinner when they see Bob walking unsteadily along the road, leaving Lundeen's. Chrissy overhears the aftermath of this incident. She lies in bed, listening to the yelling downstairs.

Chrissy drives the boat fast, but she isn't wild.

Civic Engagement

The sewer is finally being built, but the Doctor's Wife and Nancy Taylor haven't withdrawn from the public sphere. When they hear of a scheme to build an apartment complex on pilings out over the lake, they go to the county courthouse to lodge a formal complaint. It's not that they're against development, it's just that you can't just let it happen at random, with no thought to how it will impact the people and the land.

"You have to have your husband's permission to complain," the clerk says.

"Pardon?" Nancy asks.

"You're not the owners of record."

"How so?"

"You're not on the deeds."

"Who's on the deeds?"

"Dr. Hagen and Mr. Taylor. There's only room for one person's name on the line."

"And it just happened to be the men's names that made it on the forms?" Nancy asks, drawing herself taller. She is very angry. The Doctor's Wife is mad too, but she also feels herself getting the bad giggles, which in turn infect Nancy. Once the giggles strike dignity is no longer an option. The clerk looks on as Nancy and the Doctor's Wife cry with laughter.

The Doctor and the House Dog

"The Bergs are moving and Beau needs a home. Beau's not clipped like a show poodle, he's shaggy and friendly," Chrissy says at dinner.

"We don't need another dog," the Doctor's Wife says.

Chrissy forces herself to cry. "Please? Otherwise he'll have to go to the pound. He'll be murdered."

"Now, Chrissy," the Doctor says, and the Doctor's Wife knows how this will end.

"He's not eating," Chrissy says a week later, lying on her stomach on the kitchen floor trying to tempt Beau with a piece of cheddar cheese. All the other dogs lived outdoors, but since Beau had previously been a housedog it was determined—not by the Doctor's Wife—that he should continue in his ways. Poodles don't shed she was assured.

Beau turns his face away from the cheese, putting his muzzle down on his paws. "I don't understand. He loves C-H-E-E-S-E," Chrissy says. Beau is said to be so smart he understands the spelling of the word. "He's wasting away."

"He'll eat when he gets hungry," the Doctor says, but days pass and Beau doesn't eat. Under his shaggy coat he begins to shrink.

Three nights into the hunger strike, the Doctor slaps his thigh. Beau looks up at him, wagging his tail. The two go upstairs. When the Doctor's Wife goes to bed she discovers Beau curled on top of the covers. From then on, Beau sleeps on the bed every night and during the day, he accompanies the Doctor on house calls, riding in the passenger seat. The Doctor's Wife is not glad to have a new dog, but she slips him chicken when no one is looking.

The Long-distance Swim

The plan is that Chrissy will swim across the lake, and Ann will accompany her in the rowboat.

"Just don't get run over," the Doctor's Wife says as the girls bang the screen door behind themselves.

The Doctor's Wife watches from the window in the living room. The small boat makes its way toward the cove. She takes up the binoculars that rest on the table between the couch and the loveseat. All she can see is Ann rowing. Finally, the boat turns around and there are two blond heads visible, both sisters sitting in the rowboat.

When they come back, Chrissy's skin is purple.

"You're cyanotic!"

"Oh, Mom," Chrissy says, moving past her to get a cookie from the jar.

Sailing

Ann and Chrissy are in the little sailboat. Ann is the skipper for today. The wind fills the sails and the little boat leans with speed.

"Today I had to carry an amputated arm to the incinerator," Chrissy says.

Ann doesn't have much sympathy. Chrissy is lucky to work at the hospital emergency room, amputated limbs or no. Ann's job is on the early shift at the pea factory where she drops peas into a basin of water. If they sink they are grade A. If they float they are grade B. Grade B has more starch than Grade A. She starts at six in the morning and gets off at six p.m. Today, she's home early because something happened to the hoppers and the line was shut down.

"An arm is nothing. Try looking at peas all day," Ann says.

"Boo hoo. Try looking at peas all day," Chrissy repeats in a singsong voice.

Chrissy is trying to get Ann to react, but Ann's not going to do it. The wind blows briskly to the point. It's been an easy sail out from the house, but the farther they go, the harder and longer the trip back will be. In a month Ann will join Bob at Stanford. She pushes the tiller to the right to turn the boat around, forgetting to warn Chrissy. The boom swings across, smacking the top of Chrissy's head.

"You jerk!" Chrissy yells.

"It barely touched you."

"I bet I have a concussion. I saw stars!"

It's frustrating to tack from starboard to port, again and again, creeping along. Chrissy rubs her head and shoots dirty looks at Ann. The boat is heavy in proportion to the size of the sail, so if there isn't enough wind, somebody has to row. Chrissy inserts the oars into the oarlocks as Ann takes down the sail. This is done in absolute silence except for the squeaking of the oars as the boat pokes along.

"It would be easier if I got out and pushed," Chrissy says. And then she does it, paddling around to the back of the boat, where she kicks strongly. Ann jumps in the water and joins her.

Snow

Today is the second day in a row of frozen trees, icy roads, snow, and general mess. Nobody can get anywhere. Chrissy sees no reason to get out of her cozy bed, so she snuggles down into her covers, ready for a long second sleep.

"Good morning, merry sunshine, how did you wake so soon?" the Doctor's Wife comes into the room, singing in her forceful tenor.

"Go away," Chrissy says.

"You've scared the little stars away and shone away the moon!" her mother continues the rest of the chorus.

After breakfast, Chrissy sits in the nook by the window. The furnace kicks on and Chrissy sighs, looking up from her book. The snow continues to fall. She blinks, looking out the window. It's so quiet with everybody gone away to college.

Through the snow, a large shadowy figure makes its way up the driveway. Then it isn't a shape, it's Chrissy's friend Pat Rheingold riding up to the back porch on her horse.

"I got so sick of being inside and I couldn't get my car out," Pat says. "Want to go for a ride?"

Chrissy scrambles into jeans and snow boots, parka. She climbs up behind Pat, holding her around the waist. The horse is obliging, clopping, sure of foot on the snow and ice.

Housekeeping

I ask my mother's best friend from college, a Japanese-American woman originally from East L.A., what she remembers about the Hagens. "I remember Bob coming to dinner at Branner Hall when we were freshmen. I guess he was checking up on Ann."

"What else?"

"I remember visiting Lake Stevens the first time, the summer after freshman year. Your grandmother ironed the sheets."

"She what?"

"And starched them."

"She wasn't always like that," Petrea says. "Not when we were little. When we were little the house would get messy sometimes."

"And then?"

"Once John got sick she made housekeeping into an art."

Fishing

Bob says because of the situation in the world he's not going to finish his senior year. He and the Doctor cast into the river as the Doctor thinks about what Bob just said. The Doctor doesn't understand. Is this about the Vietnam War? The Doctor doesn't support the war either. One day he stood up in the staff room at Everett General and gave an anti-war speech. That didn't earn him any friends, but it was the right thing to do.

"You'll regret it if you don't finish college," the Doctor says forcefully. It is hard for him to get the words out. He still has a temper and he'd like to be able to control it. This is ridiculous. You don't go to college for three years and then drop out. The Doctor went straight to medical school after college, from there to his residency, and then to the war. He'd say this to Bob, but he doesn't like to hold himself up as an example of anything.

Bob's Side

Earlier in the spring, Bob led a march to protest the military-industrial complex. The march ended with Bob standing on the roof of the Stanford Research Institute. Later that week, the dean of admissions pronounced that no Hagen relative or progeny would ever attend Stanford again. As though it matters what a dean of admissions thinks. Bob knows a revolution is coming. When he gets back to California, he's going to enlist in the Army and volunteer to be sent to the Vietnam War so he can take the operation down from the inside.

Bob wonders if he should be fishing. It's bourgeois, or at least the way it's practiced in this family. On the other hand, he is soothed by the familiar feel of his waders, the pull of the river rushing past.

Hawaii

Spring break of her senior year in high school, Chrissy takes a trip to Hawaii with her parents. Ann and Bob have never gone and they are bitter about her trip, which is satisfying. The Hagens are traveling with the Taylors, including their two boys James and Bill, and the dentist Dr. Kirkshank and his wife. After they spend a few days in Oahu they're flying to Maui. The first night at the hotel on Waikiki Beach, Chrissy opens her windows to feel the ocean breezes while she sleeps. She's a bit hot and itchy from the bad sunburn she got that afternoon, but she's just gotten her braces off and the vacation stretches before her.

The next morning, Chrissy, Bill and James walk down the beach to the Royal Hawaiian, a massive old pink hotel where they've heard they can rent surfboards from the concession stand, a little Tiki hut. The guy who runs the place is a real surfer, gorgeously tanned. Chrissy smiles, feeling especially glad the braces are gone.

"You have to bring your board back here or you'll lose your deposit," he says.

She carries her board into the crashing waves. It is hard work getting out past the breakers, but Chrissy hasn't been swimming her whole life for nothing. She watches the locals survey the waves coming in. She's bodysurfed before, so she knows how it feels when a wave is right, how the power of the water surges the body forward onto shore.

Chrissy squints her eyes as she catches sight of a big wave. She paddles in front of it, feels the wave pick up the surfboard and then she scrambles upright. For a few glorious seconds she stands on her board before she falls back, launching the board away from her. She kicks to the surface, scans the waves for her board and when she spots it, swims for it.

"Look out, look out!" she hears. She turns around and James Taylor's surfboard whacks her right in the face. She swims in, her head pounding. When she reaches the beach she pauses to examine herself. Her teeth feel wrong and her lip is split from the inside to the outside.

"You've gotta bring your own surfboard in!" yells the attendant from the surfboard concession. Chrissy heads back to the hotel, unable to worry about him or the stupid surfboard. She tries to hold her teeth in her mouth but doesn't wipe away the blood as it gushes out.

Bill follows behind Chrissy. "We shouldn't say that James was the one who hit you, we'll say it's a stranger," he says. This seems right. This will go better if there's no one single person to blame, and even though Chrissy is the one injured, she can see that she might be accused of bringing this on herself for being such a risk-taker. Chrissy finds the adults in the hotel restaurant having lunch. The Doctor's Wife leaps up.

"She got hit by somebody's surfboard," Bill Taylor explains.

"Were you knocked unconscious?" the Doctor asks.

Chrissy shakes her head no.

"Let me see your mouth," Dr. Kirkshank says.

She shakes her head again.

"I can't do anything unless we can see."

Chrissy opens. Dr. Kirkshank pushes the loose teeth back into position. She'd like to scream, but his fingers are in the way, and all she can manage is a strangled kind of noise.

"I've got to stitch your lip up, but I need to get Novocain first," the Doctor says.

"Just do it now," Chrissy says, garbling the words. "It hurts so bad anyway."

"No, I need Novocain."

Chrissy holds ice to her lip while he's gone. It's a Sunday and it takes two hours for the Doctor to find an open pharmacy. Her sunburn from the day before suddenly becomes worse. She looks like a horrible monster, she can feel it. She won't be able to meet any boys. She won't even be able to chew the sweet pineapple she's been promised.

The Garden

The summer after her freshman year at Whitman College, Chrissy becomes Petrea. The Doctor's Wife understands why she'd want to make the change. Petrea is her given name. It sounds more grown-up.

Also that summer, what was once the swamp across the road becomes the garden. The Doctor's Wife and her husband turn the lot over with pitchforks until their hands blister. They add fertilizer, install a spigot for water. Cottonwood trees at the back of the property shield the garden from the view and sound of the Vernon Road. They raise peas, beets, onions, potatoes. Green beans and cucumbers are eaten fresh or put up in a spicy brine. They grow tomatoes, corn. The corn you can eat right from the stalk, raw in the garden.

Pronouncement

"I will too marry a black man if I want to!" Petrea yells at the conclusion of a debate with her father, loud enough for everyone else in the Golden Temple Chinese Restaurant to hear. The Doctor's Wife and her husband have always tried to encourage civic engagement and interest in the political questions of the day, so in one way you could say they are to blame.

In Law

"Are you a Marxist or a Maoist?" is the very first thing Bob says to Ann's fiancé, Carlos. It's 1972 and all the younger men wear mustaches. Bob's is blond and Carlos's mustache is black. Carlos is from El Paso, Texas. One side of his family is from Mexico and the other has been in New Mexico for four hundred years. This is what Ann told the Doctor's Wife when the Doctor's Wife asked where he came from.

The Doctor's Wife rolls out pie dough. It is a simple recipe, shortening, flour, ice water, salt, which produces a flaky crust. The filling today is wild blackberries picked from the mountains, from secret logged off spots that foragers don't share with each other. The Doctor's Wife has picked her own plenty of times, but for today's pies she ordered a gallon of berries from a friend. The berries are tartly intense and they take a lot of sugar to make the filling taste right.

"My dad and I used to eat tamales from the can," she hears Ann tell Carlos, as though explaining why this was always meant to be.

Isn't That Right?

"I've planed the bottom, but it's still jamming," the Doctor says as he opens and closes the front door, demonstrating where it sticks.

"It's so wet here in Washington. It must expand because of the moisture and then it sticks," Carlos says. He wants to impress his future father-in-law.

"So what do we do?"

"We take the door down and adjust the hinges. It's more work, but that's the only long-term solution."

"Come look at this," the Doctor says.

Carlos follows the Doctor into the kitchen. The Doctor opens and closes the spice cabinet.

"What are you doing?" the Doctor's Wife asks.

"We probably ought to work on these hinges too, isn't that right, Carlos?"

"Yes."

"Probably that's what's the matter with the upstairs shower door. Isn't that right, Carlos?"

"Are you going to finish the front door first?" the Doctor's Wife asks.

Carlos and the Doctor take the door off the hinges, walking it down the stairs, around to the big basement door. Gretel follows the two inside the basement, parking herself next to the table saw.

"Oil-based paint is a whole lot messier and a pain to deal with, but water-based paint doesn't stick to wood," says the Doctor. "Isn't that right, Carlos?"

"Yes."

"I recently repainted the south side of the house with anti-spider formula. Reduced the number of spiders by a lot. I don't know of any formula for spiders that I can put into water-based paint. For my money, I feel more comfortable with the oil-based."

Carlos gets ready to answer in the affirmative.

"Isn't that right, Gretel?" the Doctor asks.

Gretel examines her undercarriage.

Ann

The Doctor is on the phone. It's 1974 and Ann is pregnant.

"You need to go get tested, you and Carlos."

"For what?"

"To make sure your baby doesn't have what John had."

What John had? All Ann can remember is that John had bright eyes, was smart, smart, and then he didn't let go of the coffee table when he was supposed to. She remembers he was healthy and then he was dying. She doesn't remember the in-between.

"It's a genetic disease. There's a test now."

Ann and Luis drive up to the Stanford Medical Center where they have plugs of skin taken out of their arms, the fleshy part at the back of the bicep. The plug has a depth of four millimeters to get down to the subcutaneous fat so that the doctor can look for unmylenated nerve fibers and to check for the production of Asulfaditide (A). Both parents have to be carriers. If both parents are carriers, their offspring have a one-in-four chance of getting the disease.

Variety Show

The handle of the badminton racquet is my microphone. I've arranged everyone in the living room after dinner. The curtains are open to the lake. My mom holds my little brother, a baby, on the low couch on one side of the bone table. Petrea and her new husband, who happens to be Jewish and from Los Angeles, sit on the other. The Doctor sits in his moss green Danish recliner. My dad and grandmother lean forward as I give the order to the Doctor to dance around the room like an Indian. The Doctor has a tremor and even I know his health isn't good, but that will not excuse him from his act. He dances in a two-step shuffle, circling the room as he whoops with his palm in front of his mouth.

Everybody else nearly dies laughing, but I don't appreciate the hilarity. The Indian Dance is supposed to be solemn.

Toys

I'm four, my brother is two and our parents have gone away to Europe for six weeks. For the first three we stay in Lake Stevens. On the wall of the upstairs hallway, my grandmother hangs up a large world map. We jab pushpins in where our parents are expected to be, and then connect the pins with pieces of colored string. They are now supposedly taking an overnight train from Rome to Paris.

"They sleep on the train?" I ask.

"Oh yes, I've slept on lots of trains in my life," our grandmother says.

Then we climb in the car and drive to Frontier Village to pick our presents for the day. We stop by Taylor's Pharmacy then pass through to the B&M via the automatic glass door—this is a necessary and interesting part of the trip—and then we make our way to the toy aisle. I choose a sleeve of colored markers. My brother points at a bag of plastic dinosaurs. I have a vague, unexplored feeling of being spoiled.

They've Gone Shopping

I sit with my grandfather, dad, and brother in the metal boat, fishing for perch on the lake. Perch are usually far below my grandfather's standards, but he's grown worse. The clouds hang low, spitting rain. My grandfather and dad cast into the lake. My brother and I don't have fishing poles, so we sit in our raincoats, sharing the same little bench. We're too young to know what we're feeling is boredom. And then my grandfather catches a mallard duck. She flaps her wings, quacking very loudly.

I know the ducks from feeding them pieces of stale bread and, during one exciting week, the Donut-O's that my brother and I begged for and then refused to eat. It's exciting to have the duck bite us with the sharp little ridges of her bill.

My grandfather reels the duck in, wrestles her aboard and performs surgery. Once free of the hook, the duck ruffles her feathers and then flies away, low over the water, one webbed foot dragging. She settles back down in the lake, far away from us.

We are cold and damp when we get back to the house. My dad draws a hot bath for my brother and me while my grandfather builds a fire. It feels strange for the menfolk to be the only ones attending to our needs.

New Start

They had plans to buy an apartment in Seattle so that they don't have to drive home after the symphony, or Seattle Arts and Lectures, but the Doctor's Parkinson's grows worse. He also has cancer, a list of other bad things. He's not even that old. He's barely sixty.

The dining room is turned into a sick room to save the trip upstairs. The Doctor's Wife nurses him.

Old Age

Gretel lived to be twenty-four. She was never a bright dog. When I was very little she'd come close to me and then topple over, taking me down with her.

The Dusslers

I wave my hand in front of my brother's facemask and we dive down, reaching for the golf ball at the same time. We swim up, throwing the ball into the floor of the raft, where it joins the others we've already collected.

We're getting ready to dive back down again when the Dussler boys drive their big yellow ski boat very close to us. The raft bobs up and down violently. Pat Dussler's electric bullhorn squawks on.

"You nearly killed those two little boys!" she yells, the bullhorn carrying her voice from her front deck out across the lake.

My brother and I find the Dusslers endlessly captivating. For one thing, if it wasn't for them, there wouldn't be any golf balls to collect—the Dusslers knock golf balls off their lawn into the lake. Collecting the golf balls doesn't seem to interest them, so we do it, though we don't return them, we keep them in a big bucket in the canning room. The golf balls are the least of what is interesting about them.

The Dusslers are beefy, athletic boys who aren't physically afraid, even when they should be. They sometimes ride a seat-less BMX bike off the roof of the boathouse, flying into the water. Once, they drove a borrowed ski boat over a big rock and tore out the engine. Another time, while trimming a new plank on the dock, Fred Jr. and Jimmy Joe stood in the water while operating an electric saw.

Pat Dussler uses the electronic bullhorn so she can be as loud as her husband and sons. She used to work at the meat counter of the B&M before she met Fred Senior. Fred and his brother own a small local burger chain. One year they began to build what they said were stables right next to our garden. After the concrete foundation was poured, an ugly building of buff colored steel rose quickly. Once completed, there were no horses to be seen. At five in the morning, metal doors banged open, starting a day full of the noises of a truck garage. My grandmother and grandfather filed a lawsuit. The land around the lake was zoned for agricultural use, so it wasn't a clear-cut case, but the suit prevailed and the garage was torn down. Now there's a frostiness between the two families. This frostiness does not diminish our fascination—actually the opposite.

Once their ski boat is tied up, the Dussler boys stand giggling at the end of the dock.

"Hey mom," Freddie yells. My brother and I poke our heads above water and watch.

Pat is on the front porch watering her pansies.

"Hey mom," Freddie says again.

We tread water. What are they going to do?

"Hey mom," Jimmy Joe says.

She turns around. "What?" she asks into her bullhorn. The two big boys pull down their trunks and moon her, their laughs booming across the lake.

The Basement

I'm downstairs with my brother in the basement, waiting for the rain to stop so that we can swim. We've found a rattrap. I pull the crossbar back, straining against the heavy-duty spring. My brother puts a pencil on the base of the trap and then I let loose the bar. The pencil snaps in two, sending shards flying. We immediately start to look for other things we can break.

"What are you doing down there?" our grandmother calls.

"Nothing," we shout up.

Where can we find more pencils? I look around the basement. The canning room was meant for Mason jars, but is now mostly filled with toys for the beach, inner tubes, skis, buckets and shovels. On a cross beam near the door to the outside are two outboard motors, a battered army-green 10 horsepower, the other a 25 horsepower in a cream and mustard colored plastic case. Behind these are a series of cabinets crammed with other stuff—an extra badminton net, the badminton racquets, the birdies, mismatched croquet balls, a sail wrapped around itself. None of these things will fit in the trap. How badly would it hurt if we put a finger in the trap?

"Boys! Come upstairs for lunch!" we are called.

Barrow, Alaska

Bob is on a mail plane landing at the Barrow Airport. Barrow is the northernmost city on the continent, 330 miles north of the Arctic Circle. It's February and the temperature hovers around negative twenty degrees. Bob lives in Fairbanks, but even there it is so cold in the winter that Bob's German Shorthair Jed has burned his whiskers off by huddling too close to the wood burning stove.

Bob has come to Barrow to sell insurance—life, property-home, car, boat, snowmobile—because Barrow is the closest town to Prudhoe Bay, the base for the oilfields of the North Slope. Despite all the oil money around, the Barrow Airport is a simple affair, one runway, a single low building. Bob takes a taxi to the hotel, in sight of the Chukchi Sea. The houses stand on stilts and are made of unpainted plywood. Whale bones share yards with broken down cars, new snowmobiles.

He checks in to the King Eider Inn and calls his mother, as he has every day since his dad died.

"Hi, Mama," he says.

"Darling!" she replies.

Does Not Deserve A Response

My brother and I play croquet early in the morning while we wait for the Rubatinos to wake up. How can they sleep so late? We've already been up for a couple of hours.

The front lawn is uneven, sloping slightly toward the juniper hedge. Dark green spots alternate with straw-colored barrens. The Doctor's Wife doesn't think it's worth installing a sprinkler system and she certainly doesn't fertilize. Fertilizer runs straight into the lake and causes algae blooms. The Dusslers have a green lawn.

I'm aiming for my brother's croquet ball. This is my last chance to redeem myself. If I hit him, then I get two extra shots and can maybe catch up. I tap my ball. It wobbles to the left as it runs through the dewy stubble, coming to rest an inch from his ball. He clicks his ball into mine and then knocks me into the sand. I throw my mallet across the lawn.

"Let's play again," he says.

Is he kidding? I'm very angry and I stalk away down the dock, taking my shirt off, ready to go for the first swim of the day, away from the cruel wickets.

"Are you sure you don't want to play again?" my younger brother asks. "You can have a head start."

One Way

Today we're having a hot dog roast for lunch and the Rubatinos are here too. Mom is holding a pot and grandma is carrying the big wicker hamper. Spicy cowboy beans are in the pot. From the hamper comes potato chips, mustard, relish, pickles, chopped up onions, paper plates, reusable plastic spoons, marshmallows, chocolate, and graham crackers.

The hotdog skewers hang from a nail in the cabana. The skewers are sturdy pieces of metal twisted around themselves so that they form a fork at one end and a loop at the other. I'm inordinately proud of our hotdog skewers. Other people have to use coat hangers. Even my mom had to use coat hangers.

I stick the skewer into the fire so that it glows. I like to do this for two reasons. One is I like to think that I'm disinfecting the skewer. The second is that the hot dog sizzles when put on the hot metal. I prefer my hot dog burned on the outside, so it goes into the center of the fire until it is black and then into a hot dog bun with mustard and relish, no ketchup.

The fire dies down and then we make smores. My brother holds his marshmallow over the fire, patiently turning it so that it becomes a caramel color. The Rubatinos have their own varying ways of roasting the marshmallows, falling somewhere in between the extremes of my brother's method and mine. My way is the best. I stick my marshmallow close enough to the embers so that it ignites, which as far as I'm concerned is the whole point of marshmallows and fire.

My grandmother has taught us that there is always one correct way to do things.

A Birthday Party

My brother and I walk back from the lake, carrying the rubber raft on our heads, our towels draped over our shoulders. Everybody is here tonight, my mom and dad, Petrea and her husband and little daughters, Bob and his second wife. We've converged from up and down the West Coast, California, Oregon, and Alaska. My brother and I are the last up from the lake. We walk under the front deck to the door to the basement. We drop the raft off inside. Children are not allowed to come from the beach through the front door and across the carpet, nor are we allowed to walk upstairs from the basement, so we make our way along the side of the house, up the little steps and on the walkway below the willow tree. A small, square, metal plate with a finger hole rests over the pipe to the heating oil tank. I step on this metal plate so that it makes a noise as it shifts from one side to the other. I can't walk on this side of the house and not step on the plate. It's a rule I have.

Across from the garage and carport my grandmother is dead-heading roses. She's wearing gardening gloves and holds clippers in her right hand. A bucket for the detritus rests on the blacktop. These are large roses, fat variegated, red, pink and peach, height of summer sun open.

"Come give this flower a sniff. It's called Fragrant Cloud."

I put my nose in the middle of it. My feet are in a warm puddle. Grandma turns back to her work.

My brother and I hose our sandy legs off with the spray attachment that prickles. At a party one is generally expected to take a shower and put on clothes. Shoes are not absolutely necessary, but a clean pair of pants and a shirt is. I take a shower and then take my time, lying on my bed naked, reading my book from the stack of books we checked out from the Everett library. My brother and I share what is now referred to as the dormitory room but that used to be my mother's room. The beds my mother and aunt Petrea carved their names into are long gone. Twin beds flank a nightstand. On the wall hangs an oval mirror in a wooden frame, a tile with a duck on it, and a drawing of a gnarled oak tree. Petrea did the pen and ink drawing. She's still considered the artistic one of the family.

I hear grandma downstairs in the kitchen with Petrea and mom, getting dinner ready.

The adults are all showered and dressed when I go downstairs. The men pull the grill out from under the carport to cook the steaks. It's mom's birthday so hors d'oeuvres are in the living room. We have cheese and olives, but also Cheetohs in a Havilland bowl. The Cheetohs are a sort of a joke granny has made. The adults drink Champagne and the kids have Martinelli's in flutes. We eat dinner on the front porch, looking out over the rhododendron bushes to the lake. The umbrella is up to block the still bright sun. The adults drink their white wine.

"That's nasty," my brother says, pointing at a loud motorboat flying across the lake. It's slim, sitting close to the surface of the water. The back sprouts what looks like a jet engine, and the boat is piloted by a bearded man wearing a Speedo. He doesn't even have anybody skiing behind him. We find him and his boat guilty on serious charges of sensibility and good taste. We don't have our own ski boat, so our scorn is mixed with jealousy.

"What's wrong with English?" Bob asks, as the adults grow quiet. My brother and I turn our attention to the conversation.

"What do you mean?" my mom asks slowly.

"It seems to work for an awful lot of people."

"How about my students? They shouldn't have to give up their Spanish. They should be supported so they know more than one language."

"Why would you want to keep learning the language you've been trying to forget?" Bob asks.

"Maybe they don't want to forget," my mother replies.

"Why would anybody want to speak anything other than English?" Bob asks. "It's in their own best interests to only speak English."

"Look, Bob, there's all sorts of research that shows that you don't have to give up your first language to learn English. Why wouldn't you want to know more than one language?"

"English works. What's wrong with it?"

"You've got to be kidding me!"

"I mean, aren't we all the same? Why can't we all speak the same language?"

"It's not that simple."

"I think it emphasizes the differences."

Bob's new wife, Petrea's husband, and my dad stay out of it.

"You live in Alaska, you don't know what it's like in the rest of the country," Petrea says.

"We live differently in Alaska. There's no racism in Alaska."

"What about the Alaskan native languages? Once those are lost we're never getting them back. That doesn't worry you?" my mom asks.

"I think it would be better if we all spoke English. Then we could communicate better with each other."

"You just don't understand, do you?"

"Don't understand what?"

"You don't understand how hard it can be for people," my mother says, growing louder.

"You girls, you're just do-gooders. We've got too many do-gooders trying to change things in this country that don't need changing."

"Well, insurance companies are ruining this country," my grandmother jumps in.

"Do you want me to be a do-gooder too?" Bob asks the group.

"You think that's all I am?" asks my mother.

"I don't want to be a social worker. I don't think that helps anything."

"You're such an asshole!" my mom says through gritted teeth. She begins crying, jerking herself up from the table and taking her plate with her into the kitchen.

Bob clomps down the outside stairs. My brother and I start to take dishes in to the kitchen, where my mom is still crying, loading the dishwasher.

"How can he believe that shit?" asks Petrea when she comes in, taking a dishrag from the drying cabinet next to the sink.

"I don't fucking know," says my mother. Bob enters through the back door.

"I'm sorry girls," he says, touching his sister's shoulders. "I didn't mean to make anybody cry."

"That's OK. I think you're right Bob," Petrea says.

"I'm right?" he asks. His deep voice lilts up.

"Yeah, why don't we just cut out people's tongues if they try and speak Spanish?" Petrea asks. "That would solve the problem, right?"

"Hee hee hee," is the way Bob laughs. He's a giant, six feet six inches and two hundred and forty pounds. His eyes squint as he shakes. When he laughs he really goes for it.

Fixing the Dock

My brother and I drive with Bob to the concrete yard in Everett to buy the ten-inch sewer pipes we'll use to fix the dock's rotting pilings. The wooden pilings don't rot underwater, so only the tops have to be cut off. After Bob cuts the rot off, we'll cap the piling with the sewer pipe and then we'll make forms out of tarpaper. The forms will be filled with cement up to the crossbeams of the dock.

Bob stands in the deep water sawing down a piling while my brother and I transport the pipes from the car, pushing the wheelbarrow down the lawn to the cabana and then down to the end of the dock. Bob gets out of the water. The wind howls. I shiver in my t-shirt and swimming trunks. Bob takes a green length of rope to make a noose to go around the pipe so that we can ease it down into position. As we're lowering it down, the pipe slips out of the noose and sinks to the bottom of the lake. Somebody will have to dive to get it.

Bob jumps in, facemask on. He is a sea mammal glowing under water, tugging at the rope, bringing his arms around the pipe and then pushing off the bottom, lifting the pipe to the surface where he slips it over the top of the piling.

I don't care for this kind of work. Why can't the my grandmother hire somebody to take care of this for us? She agrees with us, imploring Bob to stop.

"I'll just replace the pilings a few at a time," Bob says.

More Work on the Dock

One summer while I'm still at Stanford, I call to ask the Doctor's Wife if I can bring a friend. My friend Namazzi is from Uganda by way of Deerfield and Stanford. Her three brothers are scattered around New England and Europe at boarding schools. She has a long neck, her hair is twisted into tiny inch-long braids, she has a wide nose, and is very beautifully, evenly, deep dark brown in the way that hardly anybody is evenly anything. Her grandmother's uncle was the king of Uganda.

"You invite whoever you want. We've had all kinds come here," the Doctor's Wife says, unimpressed when I tell her Namazzi's family history.

That summer we also spend a few days working on the dock, replacing the planking near the cabana. Namazzi works along with the rest of us, wielding a hammer.

"Oh, we've even had royalty visit," I hear my grandmother say casually, a couple of years later.

The Freezer

"I hate to think about what to fix for breakfast. I never know what people want," my grandmother says to me.

"Can't they get their own breakfasts?" I ask. I'm here before an invasion of the other family members. I flatter myself by thinking I'm here to help.

"Do people want eggs?" she asks.

"You don't want eggs."

"No, I don't want eggs," she says shuddering. "What should we have for breakfast this morning?"

"Cereal?"

"Hmm, I bought a quart of half-and-half but I forgot milk," she says, looking in the refrigerator.

"I'll have toast."

"No, we'll eat our cereal with cream. Everybody puts cream on cereal," she says grandly. Everybody does not do this. We eat our cereal in quiet, blissful concentration.

"I have cinnamon rolls in the freezer," she says, after we've licked the last drops of cream from our spoons. She has a full-sized freezer on the utility porch that holds pounds of butter, homemade chicken stock, salmon, wild blackberries, ice cream, nuts, butter, lamb chops, whole casseroles, and pies. When I was little I had access to a limitless supply of Fudgesicles, Otter Pops in lurid colors, strawberry yogurt Push-Ups.

She has been known to freeze garbage. "Everybody freezes garbage," I've heard her say. "What else are you supposed to do with fish remains on Saturday and you don't want them stinking up the garbage cans?"

"Do you think the cinnamon rolls will be OK for breakfasts?" she asks.

"Of course they'll be OK," I say. "My dad will eat a whole package by himself."

To make the rolls she mixes the ingredients into a sticky dough, separating it into medium-sized balls. The dough rises and she punches it down a couple of times before using a rolling pin to flatten the balls into long rectangles. She shakes a cinnamon and sugar mixture over the surface, drops raisins on one edge, tucks dough over the edge with the raisins, continuing to roll until she has a log that she cuts into pieces. She lines the rolls up in a buttered Pyrex dish. The process usually begins in the early morning, continuing into the middle of the afternoon.

"I'm essentially a lazy person," she explains, maybe even believing that this could be true. "I don't mind doing anything if I can do it ahead of time."

Attention

My mom and I have tricked my grandmother into staying down at the lake while we make salmon salad sandwiches from last night's leftovers. We mix the grilled fish with chopped up celery, mayonnaise, dill and then spread butter thick on the bread, topping the sandwiches with lettuce and tomatoes from Carleton's farm stand. I get a bag of chips from the bin kept on the utility porch and then load up a tray with iced tea, the sandwiches, and chips, to take down to the lake to my boyfriend Matthew, my grandmother, Petrea, and Petrea's almost all-grown-up daughters, my cousins.

The cousins wait until the last possible moment to come out from the sun and under the shade of the cabana. They are trying to get as dark as they can this summer. The older girl cousin is a scientist about to go UCSF for her PhD in immunology, but this summer she's working as an accountant for G.I. Joe's, a sporting goods store in Frontier Village. Frontier Village has outgrown its original confines, eating into the woods on all sides.

The other cousin, in college, has been helping my grandmother organize the basement this summer. There have been several battles about how things should go. No one in this family could be accused of not having an opinion. Both of the cousins' jobs allow them to work in the morning and then sun and swim in the afternoon.

As I set down the tray, I sense an odd sort of stillness. My brother and Petrea are reading. Matthew gives me a look like he wants to talk to me.

"I forgot to bring cups," I say. "Matthew, do you want to help me?"

"Your aunt Petrea kicked me," he says as we walk up the lawn.

"That means she likes you."

"It hurt," he says. "I think I'm going to have a bruise."

"Really, if she didn't like you she'd just ignore you."

"How old is she?"

"You know what my great-grandmother Petie used to say?"

"What?"

"The older we get the more like ourselves we become."

He isn't impressed by this family saying.

The Summer We Cry

Bob's leg has been hurting and so after limping around for six weeks, he visits his doctor. It turns out the leg is broken. It broke because he's riddled with cancer. This is in June of 2002.

In July, I stand in the kitchen with my arms around my grandmother, feeling strange to be crying so plainly. I'm not a crier, but the tears come hot and fast. My parents are in Italy for a month and a decision had been made not to ruin their trip. They are to be told how sick Bob is when they come back.

When Bob was in college and tried to enlist, he was rejected by the army because the FBI had put a red flag on his file. After he graduated from college, he moved to East Oakland, where he joined a Socialist Worker's Party commune. He was a labor organizer, took lots of LSD and was even arrested once. After he left the commune, he found a job at a big insurance company in San Francisco. He met Eve, an Arapajo aeronautical engineer who worked at Boeing. Together, they went deep into the philosophy of Gurdjieff, hoping to reach a higher level of consciousness.

Something about the Gurdjieffian rejection of modernity and, I'm sure, the incomparable hunting and fishing, brought Bob and Eve to Fairbanks, Alaska, where Bob became a Republican, and Eve an alcoholic. When their marriage ended, Bob, like many others in the state, became a Libertarian. Alaskans refer to the rest of the world as The Outside, a term that even the big Anchorage newspaper uses.

Bob hunted ptarmigan and ducks, fished for King salmon, married again, opened his own successful insurance agency, and when he was fifty, he adopted Native Alaskan twins. He'd seemed settled and happy finally.

Over the course of the summer Bob grows worse and worse. At the beginning of August, my mom and brother fly to Alaska to spend time with him and to help his wife out with the boys. My brother and Bob talk about God, the Christian God, because Bob has just joined the Presbyterian Church. My brother is in divinity school at Yale, on the academic rather than priestly track. Bob has thrown himself into Christianity like he's thrown himself into everything else. He subscribes to a journal called the *Biblical Archeology Review*.

In late August, he's in the hospital. My mother calls me to tell me the latest. Earlier in the day Bob jumped out of his hospital bed, stood up, drew himself to his true height, not the shrunken size he'd become, and ripped out his IV line, loudly demanding that he be allowed to die. This performance badly scared the nurse, who sent a psychiatrist, who had a long private talk with Bob. After the talk, the psychiatrist said that Bob was perfectly sane. Bob and the psychiatrist had already had the same conversation a couple of weeks before, agreeing that when Bob knew that there was no more hope, he'd refuse treatment.

"I'll book a ticket," I tell my mom.

I've never been to Alaska, though Bob has invited us all many times before. His house is up on a hill overlooking the city of Anchorage on one side and on the other, the Chugach Peninsula's sandy hook, curving around Cook's Inlet. In the winter the winds blow ninety miles an hour. But the afternoon I arrive it is a sunny, warm day. Moments after I've carried in my luggage, a moose ambles into the yard to eat petunias from the flower borders. The dogs are kept inside so the moose doesn't gore them. They go crazy, flinging themselves against the glass in the door.

When the moose leaves, my mom takes me to see Bob at the hospital. He's alert enough to thank me for coming to Alaska, but he soon drifts into an uneasy kind of sleep.

For dinner we cook a salmon that Bob's wife caught earlier in the day from Ship Creek downtown. The sun sets at eleven. The next morning, Bob isn't talking anymore. He is deep inside himself, sometimes crying out. I can see the tumors under the skin of his chest and legs.

We don't know what else to do, so we sing. Even though most of us aren't religious, we sing hymns and spirituals, *Swing Low, Sweet Chariot, Morning Has Broken, Nearer My God to Thee*. I sing low, my grandmother takes the tenor parts and the two sisters sing up high. We absentmindedly work crossword puzzles. We play Bach cello sonatas on a little boom box my grandmother bought at Fred Meyer. When we feel restless, we leave the oncology wing and wander the halls, looking at the Native Alaskan artwork scattered around the hospital.

One afternoon, Petrea cries and cries, unable to stop herself. My grandmother and I leave to go back to the house to get dinner ready. On the way to the car, my grandmother is fiercely calm. "Why is Petrea crying? She needs to stop. She doesn't know what it is to lose two sons," she says.

After three days of watching Bob try to die, three days of going to the hospital in shifts, three days of trips to the cafeteria for coffee and sandwiches, three days of going back to the house to ride bikes with the little boys, after three days of a horrible sort of waiting, a woman wearing a flowy gown and carrying a large velvet bag walks in to the hospital room. She takes a harp out of her velvet bag.

"Would you mind if I play for him?" she asks.

"He loves music," my grandmother says. "Can you play any Mozart?"

"I usually play something that people don't know so they can't listen for a tune. That way they can forget what they're doing." What she means is that they forget to hold on to life. She starts plucking the strings. I feel like I should stay in the room, but I haven't really slept for days and all I can think about is going to the small waiting room at the end of the hall and stretching out on one of the vinyl couches. From the couch I can still hear the strumming and I lie there, suspended between waking and dreaming.

Then my mother is next to me. "Come with me," she says, hustling me back to Bob's room. Looking down at his body I can tell he isn't there.

"Thank you," we say to the harpist.

The woman gives us her card as she leaves. Under her name is printed her profession, "Thanatologist."

"What's a thanatologist?" my mom asks when the woman leaves.

"I think thanatos is another kind of time," I answer. "There's thanatos and chronos. Chronos is regular time, chronological time, and thanatos is something else—I'm not sure what."

"You're so smart," my mom says, but she's wrong. What I'm good at is sounding like I know what I'm talking about. I've only got it partially right. The counterpart to the earthly time of Chronos is Kairos, the time of the gods. Thanatos is the personification of death in Greek myth and, linguistically anyway, has nothing to do with time.

Religion

"What part of the bible did you talk to Bob about?" I ask my brother.

"We read the Book of Luke together."

"For any particular reason?"

"According to tradition, Luke was a physician. The text of Luke is often concerned with healing and reconciliation. You can tell it has that emphasis because of how it differs from Mark and Matthew."

"What do you mean?"

"These three gospels have the same parables, but they don't quite match up either chronologically or in the details."

"What's an example?" I ask. Details and emphasis always change with the storyteller.

"In Matthew, Jesus preaches the Sermon on the Mount. In Luke, he preaches the Sermon on the *Plain* because he hasn't reached the mountain yet."

She Began College at Fifteen

"What's going on here?" I ask my grandmother, pointing at a close-up picture of my grandfather and his twin brother. They're both wearing fedoras, suits and ties, but they also look a little drunk. The inscription in the album is in white ink on black paper and reads, "Union Station—Early one Sunday morning after med. school party—Taggie and D. slept at Normie's."

"Are you D?" I ask. The Doctor's Wife's name is Doris.

"Yes."

Who were Taggie and Normie?"

"They were sorority sisters, good friends. True blue Kansas characters."

"What kinds of names are those?"

"Taggie was Joanne Taggart and Normie was Norma Jean Faulkner. But we also had nicknames."

"Nicknames for the nicknames?"

"Norm the Form, Tag the Bag, Dor the—well, you know."

One Story Leads to the Next

My family accuses me of leaving out a lot of the best stories.

"What else would I put in?" I ask my mom. "There's the story about Bob sticking his tongue out and the snapping turtle grabbed hold of it. I could put that in."

"Oh yeah. Here's something. I remember when Dad was really sick with Parkinson's and he told me that the one thing he regretted was saying 'Swim goddamn it!' to Bob when he fell in that water that time. I think dad thought it may have had something to do with why they couldn't see eye to eye."

"What did you say to Grandpa Bob when he told you that?"

"I was speechless, but then I said, 'It's OK, Dad,' or something like that. Oh, and then there was the time that Bob got a shotgun out of the gun closet in the basement."

"What happened exactly?"

"Bob joined the mountain rescue squad. One day we had a big storm and Bob got a call to do a rescue up on Mount Pilchuck. He called the office to ask Dad if he could go and Dad said no. Bob got really mad and he went down the basement for a gun. Mom called Dad and the office and then Dad came home."

"And then what happened? What did Grandpa Bob do?"

"And then it's hazy. That's all I remember."

"Anything else?"

"You have to put in the story about John's urine sample."

But this is a story my grandmother just let out, it's not a family story. Once when John was really sick he had to be strapped to a hospital bed for twenty-four hours to collect urine samples. My grandparents left him overnight and then in the morning, when John was almost ready to be released a nurse knocked the sample to the floor.

I press my grandmother for details.

"So the samples were in glass bottles?"

"I don't remember."

"Did you take him back to do the tests over?"

"No, I think your grandfather decided that John shouldn't have to go through that again."

"Were you mad at the nurse?"

"I wanted to kill her. But she must have felt awful too."

Dumb Luck

"It's all dumb luck," the Doctor's Wife says, explaining her new theory to my mother. I've already heard the theory.

"What's dumb luck?" asks my mom.

"Life. It's all dumb luck."

"Don't you think that genetics has something to do with it?"

"Genetics is dumb luck."

"What about education?"

"Dumb luck."

"That's not what you thought when you were younger."

"Of course I did," the Doctor's Wife snorts.

"It was not dumb luck whether or not I got good grades. I was expected to study. Is it dumb luck if you study and then get good grades?"

"Well," the Doctor's Wife says. "It's dumb luck that you had the sort of parents who made you study."

They work quietly for a while, cutting up the pieces of apple, getting ready for the others to come.

"Aren't we lucky?" the Doctor's Wife asks.

Acknowledgments

I'd like to thank the editors of *Tin House*, where "The Pacific War" first appeared. Thank you to the editors of *HOW Journal*, where slightly different versions of several stories appeared including, "The Bone Table"; "Table Manners"; "A Nurse Doll"; "Afraid of the Dark"; "A Sense of Humor"; "More Tests"; "Home"; "Seizures"; and "There's Nothing Bad That Can't Get Worse."

Thank you to my dear writing friends Alison Hart, Heather Abel, and the incomparable Abigail Thomas. Thank you to Rebecca Reilly, Lisa Freedman, Leah Iannone, Kathryne Squilla, Lori Lynn Turner, and Laura Cronk. Thanks also to Catherine Luttinger, Mira Jacob, Shelley Salamensky, Sarah Bardin, John Pappas and Sufjan Stevens. Thank you to Sara Lamm, Jon Raymond, John Reed, and Andrew Zornoza.

Thank you to Robert Polito, Hilton Als and Zia Jaffrey for your mentorship. Thank you to Helen Schulman, Tiphanie Yanique, and all the rest of my inspiring and supportive friends and colleagues at The New School. Thank you to the many students over the years who have taught me so much.

Thank you to Ira Silverberg for his support. Thank you to Dan Wickett and Matt Bell for their thoughtful edits and for being such good friends to writers. Thank you to Ethan Bassoff for his sharp eye and sharper mind. Thank you to Eve Turow for her tireless efforts.

Thank you to Nancy Mitchell, Darwin Smith, the Volpones, and the people of Lake Stevens. Thank you to my family—the Jaramillos, the Hagens, and Gildens—for their help with this book, and to Matthew Brookshire, who makes everything possible.

Luis Jaramillo has had short stories published in *Open City* and *Tin House*. He is the Associate Chair of the New School Writing Program, where he teaches fiction and nonfiction.